W9-CJZ-379

John and Lorraine are two young people looking for a way out of the numbness of being
lonely. What they find are each other, and the
Pigman. What they create out of their zaniness
and energy is a laughter and a love too good
to last . . .

THE PIGMAN

"Headline news . . . remarkable . . . Zindel has
written a story that will not be denied."

—*Publishers Weekly*

"This is a shocker of a book, written in a con-
temporary idiom. It is a haunting story. The
book is startling and truthful and vivid."

—*Young Readers' Review*

PAUL ZINDEL, the famous novelist and play-
wright, is the author of MY DARLING, MY
HAMBURGER; CONFESSIONS OF A TEEN-
AGE BABOON; I NEVER LOVED YOUR
MIND; and PARDON ME, YOU'RE STEPPING
ON MY EYEBALL! as well as the Pulitzer Prize-
winning drama, THE EFFECT OF GAMMA
RAYS ON MAN-IN-THE-MOON MARI-
GOLDS.

Bantam Books by Paul Zindel
Ask your bookseller for the books you have missed

CONFESSIONS OF A TEENAGE BABOON
THE EFFECT OF GAMMA RAYS ON
  MAN-IN-THE-MOON MARIGOLDS
I NEVER LOVED YOUR MIND
MY DARLING, MY HAMBURGER
PARDON ME, YOU'RE STEPPING ON MY
  EYEBALL!
THE PIGMAN
THE PIGMAN'S LEGACY
A STAR FOR THE LATECOMER
  (with Bonnie Zindel)
THE UNDERTAKER'S GONE BANANAS

Paul Zindel
The Pigman

MADONNA COLLEGE
LIBRARY
Livonia, Michigan

CHILD LT
PS
3576
.I 518
P5
1981

BANTAM BOOKS
TORONTO · NEW YORK · LONDON · SYDNEY

109531

This low-priced Bantam Book
has been completely reset in a type face
designed for easy reading, and was printed
from new plates. It contains the complete
text of the original hard-cover edition.
NOT ONE WORD HAS BEEN OMITTED.

RL 6, IL 6+

THE PIGMAN

A Bantam Book / published by arrangement with
Harper & Row Publishers, Inc.

PRINTING HISTORY

Harper & Row edition published March 1968

2nd printing	March 1969	6th printing	October 1973
3rd printing	May 1969	7th printing ..	December 1974
4th printing	May 1970	8th printing	January 1977
5th printing ..	November 1971	9th printing	January 1978

Bantam edition / December 1978

2nd printing	July 1979	5th printing	January 1981
3rd printing	April 1980	6th printing	February 1981
4th printing	October 1980	7th printing	July 1981

All rights reserved.
Copyright © 1968 by Paul Zindel.
Cover art copyright © 1981 by Bantam Books, Inc.
This book may not be reproduced in whole or in part, by
mimeograph or any other means, without permission.
For information address: Harper & Row Publishers, Inc.,
10 East 53rd Street, New York, N.Y. 10022.

ISBN 0-553-14657-2

Published simultaneously in the United States and Canada

Bantam Books are published by Bantam Books, Inc. Its trademark, consisting of the words "Bantam Books" and the por-
trayal of a rooster, is Registered in U.S. Patent and Trademark
Office and in other countries. Marca Registrada. Bantam
Books, Inc., 666 Fifth Avenue, New York, New York 10103.

PRINTED IN THE UNITED STATES OF AMERICA

16 15 14 13 12 11 10 9 8 7

FOR
the Boy and Girl of Stapleton

The Oath

Being of sound mind and body on this 15th day of April in our sophomore year at Franklin High School, let it be known that Lorraine Jensen and John Conlan have decided to record the facts, and only the facts about our experiences with Mr. Angelo Pignati.

Miss Reillen, the Cricket, is watching us at every moment because she is the librarian at Franklin High and thinks we're using her typewriter to copy a book report for our retarded English teacher.

The truth and nothing but the truth, until this memorial epic is finished, So Help Us God!

John Conlan

Lorraine Jensen

g your lungs with that funny... was
out of her mouth... inhaled a deep
...ed puff from my cigarette. She stared
...her when she saw that.

The Pigman

1

Now, I don't like school, which you might say is one
of the factors that got us involved with this old guy
we nicknamed the Pigman. Actually, I hate school,
but then again most of the time I hate everything.

I used to really hate school when I first started at
Franklin High. I hated it so much the first year
they called me the Bathroom Bomber. Other kids got
elected G.O. President and class secretary and lab-
squad captain, but I got elected the Bathroom Bomber. They called me that because I used to set off
bombs in the bathroom. I set off twenty-three bombs
before I didn't feel like doing it anymore.

The reason I never got caught was because I used
to take a tin can (that's a firecracker, as if you didn't
know) and mold a piece of clay around it so it'd hold
a candle attached to the fuse. One of those skinny
little birthday candles. Then I'd light the thing, and
it'd take about eight minutes before the fuse got lit.
I always put the bombs in the first-floor boys' john
right behind one of the porcelain unmentionables
where nobody could see it. Then I'd go off to my
next class. No matter where I was in the building
I could hear the blast.

If I got all involved, I'd forget I had lit the bomb,

and then even I'd be surprised when it went off. Of course, I was never as surprised as the poor guys who were in the boys' john on the first floor sneaking a cigarette, because the boys' john is right next to the Dean's office and a whole flock of gestapo would race in there and blame them. Sure they didn't do it, but it's pretty hard to say you're innocent when you're caught with a lungful of rich, mellow tobacco smoke. When the Dean catches you smoking, it really may be hazardous to your health. I smoke one with a recessed filter myself.

After my bomb avocation, I became the organizer of the supercolossal fruit roll. You could only do this on Wednesdays because that was the only day they sold old apples in the cafeteria. Sick, undernourished, antique apples. They sold old oranges on Fridays, but they weren't as good because they don't make much noise when you roll them. But on Wednesdays when I knew there was going to be a substitute teaching one of the classes, I'd pass the word at lunch and all the kids in that class would buy these scrawny apples. Then we'd take them to class and wait for the right moment—like when the substitute was writing on the blackboard. You couldn't depend on a substitute to write on the blackboard though, because usually they just told you to take a study period so they didn't have to do any work and could just sit at the desk reading *The New York Times*. But you could depend on the substitute to be mildly retarded, so I'd pick out the right moment and clear my throat quite loudly—which was the signal for everyone to get the apples out. Then I gave this phony sneeze that meant to hold them down near the floor. When I whistled, that was the signal to roll 'em. Did you ever hear a herd of buffalo stampeding? Thirty-four scrawny, undernourished apples rolling up the aisles sound just like a herd of buffalo stampeding.

Every one of the fruit rolls was successful, except for the time we had a retired postman for General Science 1H5. We were supposed to study incandescent lamps, but he spent the period telling us about commemorative stamps. He was so enthusiastic about the old days at the P.O. I just didn't have the heart to give the signals, and the kids were a little put out because they all got stuck with old apples.

But I gave up all that kid stuff now that I'm a sophomore. The only thing I do now that is faintly criminal is write on desks. Like right this minute I feel like writing something on the nice polished table here, and since the Cricket is down at the other end of the library showing some four-eyed dimwit how to use the encyclopedias, I'm going to do it.

HELP ME !!!
A ROTTEN science
TEACHER has given me a drug
to

change me into a
teeny weeny
mosquito ...
please help me ...
I'm melting ...

Now that I've artistically expressed myself, we might as well get this cursing thing over with too.

I was a little annoyed at first since I was the one who suggested writing this thing because I couldn't stand the miserable look on Lorraine's face ever since the Pigman died. She looked a little bit like a Saint Bernard that just lost its keg, but since she agreed to work on this, she's gotten a little livelier and more opinionated. One of her opinions is that I shouldn't curse.

"Not in a memorial epic!"

"Let's face it," I said, "everyone curses."

She finally said I could curse if it was excruciatingly necessary by going like this @#$%. Now that isn't too bad an idea because @#$% leaves it to the imagination and most people have a worse imagination than I have. So I figure I'll go like @#$% if it's a mild curse—like the kind you hear in the movies when everyone makes believe they're morally violated but have really gotten the thrill of a lifetime. If it's going to be a revolting curse, I'll just put a three in front of it—like 3@#$%—and then you'll know it's the raunchiest curse you can think of.

Just now I'd better explain why we call Miss Reillen the Cricket. Like I told you, she's the librarian at Franklin and is letting us type this thing on her quiet typewriter, which isn't quiet at all. But there aren't many kids in seventh-period study because most of them cut it and the others get excused early because our school is overcrowded. It's only kids like Lorraine and me that get stuck with seventh-period study because we have to stay around for an eighth-period class called Problems in American Democracy. And if you think having Problems in American Democracy is a fun way to end the day, you need a snug-fitting straitjacket.

Anyway, Miss Reillen is a little on the fat side, but that doesn't stop her from wearing these tight skirts which make her nylon stockings rub together when she walks so she makes this scraaaaaaatchy sound. That's why the kids call her the Cricket. If she taught woodshop or gym, nobody'd really know she makes that sound—but she's the librarian, and it's so quiet you can hear every move she makes.

Lorraine is panting to get at the typewriter now, so I'm going to let her before she has a heart attack.

2

I should never have let John write the first chapter because he always has to twist things subliminally. I am not panting, and I'm not about to have a thrombosis. It's just that some very strange things have happened to us during the last few months, and we feel we should write them down while they're fresh in our minds. It's got to be written now before John and I mature and repress the whole thing.

John doesn't really curse that much, and I don't think he needs his system. But even when we were in Miss Stewart's typing class, he had to do something unusual all the time—like type a letter in the shape of an hourglass. That's the kind of thing he does. And as you probably suspected, the reason John gets away with all these things is because he's extremely handsome. I hate to admit it, but he is. An ugly boy would have been sent to reform school by now.

He's six feet tall already, with sort of longish brown hair and blue eyes. He has these gigantic eyes that look right through you, especially if he's in the middle of one of his fantastic everyday lies. And he drinks and smokes more than any boy I ever heard of. The analysts would call his family the source problem or say he drinks and smokes to assert his independence.

I tried to explain to him how dangerous it was, particularly smoking, and even went to the trouble of finding a case history similar to his in a book by Sigmund Freud. I almost had him convinced that smoking was an infantile, destructive activity when he pointed out a picture of Freud smoking a cigar on the book's cover.

"If Freud smokes, why can't I?"

"Freud doesn't smoke anymore," I told him. "He's dead."

Another time I got my mother to bring home a pamphlet about smoking in which they showed lungs damaged from tobacco poisons. I even got her to borrow a book from a doctor, which had large color plates of lungs that had been eaten away by cancer. She's a nurse and can get all those things. But nothing seems to have any impact on John, which I suppose brings us right back to his source problem. Actually, we both have families you wouldn't believe, but I don't particularly feel like going into it at the moment because I just ate lunch in the cafeteria. It was Swiss steak. That is, they called it Swiss steak. John called it filet of gorilla's heart.

Also, you'll find out soon enough that John distorts—when he isn't out-and-out lying. For example, in Problems in American Democracy the other day, Mr. Weiner asked him what kind of homes early American settlers lived in, and John said tree huts. Now John knows early American settlers didn't live in tree huts, but he'll do just about anything to stir up some excitement. And he really did set off those bombs when he was a freshman, which when you stop to consider sort of shows a pattern—an actual pattern. I think he used to distort things physically, and now he does it verbally more than any other way.

I mean take the Cricket for instance. I mean Miss
Reillen. She's across the library watching me as I'm
typing this, and she's smiling. You'd think she knew
I was defending her. She's really a very nice woman,
though it's true her clothes are too tight, and her
nylons do make this scraaaaaaatchy sound when she
walks. But she isn't trying to be sexy or anything. If
you could see her, you'd know that. She just outgrew
her clothes. Maybe she doesn't have any money to
buy new ones or get the old ones let out. Who knows
what kind of problems she has? Maybe she's got a
sick mother at home like Miss Stewart, the typing
teacher. I know Miss Stewart has a sick mother
because she had me mark some typing papers illegally
and drop them off at her house after school one day.
And there was her sick mother—very thin and with
this smile frozen on her face—right in the middle
of the living room! That was the strange part. Miss
Stewart kept her mother in this bed right in the
middle of the living room, and it almost made me
cry. She made a little joke sbout it—how she kept
her mother in the middle of the living room because
she didn't want her to think she was missing anything
when people came to visit. Can you imagine keeping
your sick mother in a bed right smack in the middle
of the living room? When I look at Miss Reillen I
feel sorry. When I hear her walking I feel even more
sorry for her because maybe she keeps her mother
in a bed in the middle of the living room just like
Miss Stewart. Who would want to marry a woman
that keeps her sick mother in a bed right in the
middle of the living room?

The one big difference between John and me, besides the fact that he's a boy and I'm a girl, is I have
compassion. Not that he really doesn't have any com-

passion, but he'd be the last one on earth to show it. He pretends he doesn't care about anything in the world, and he's always ready with some outrageous remark, but if you ask me, any real hostility he has is directed against himself.

The fact that I'm his best friend shows he isn't as insensitive to *Homo sapiens* as he makes believe he is, because you might as well know I'm not exactly the most beautiful girl in the world. I'm not Venus or Harlow. Just ask my mother.

"You're not a pretty girl, Lorraine," she has been nice enough to inform me on a few occasions (as if I didn't remember the first time she ever said it), "but you don't have to walk about stoop-shouldered and hunched." At least once a day she fills me in on one more aspect of my public image—like "your hair would be better cut short because it's too kinky," and "you're putting on too much weight," and "you wear your clothes funny." If I made a list of every comment she's made about me, you'd think I was a monstrosity. I may not be Miss America, but I am not the abominable snowwoman either.

But as I was saying, it is a fact that John has compassion deep inside of him, which is the real reason we got involved with the Pigman. Maybe at first John thought of it all simply as a way of getting money for beer and cigarettes, but the second we met the old man, John changed, even though he won't admit it. As a matter of fact, it was this very compassion that made John finally introduce himself to me and invite me for a beer in Moravian Cemetery. He always went to Moravian Cemetery to drink beer, which sounds a little crazy, but it isn't if you explore his source problem a bit. Although I didn't know John and his family until two years ago when I moved into the neighborhood, from what I've been able to gather I think his father was a compulsive alcoholic. I've spent hours trying to analyze the situation, and the closest I've been able to come to a theory is that his father set a bad example at an age when John was impressionable. I think his father made it seem as though drinking alcoholic beverages was a sign of maturity. This particular sign of maturity ended up giving his father sclerosis of the liver, so he doesn't drink anymore, but John does.

I had moved into John's neighborhood at the start of my freshman year, and he and a bunch of other kids used to wait for the same bus I did on the corner of Victory Boulevard and Eddy Street. I was in a severe state of depression the first few weeks because no one spoke to me. It wasn't that I was expecting the boys to buzz around and ask me out, but I was sort of hoping that at least one of the girls would be friendly enough to borrow a hairpin or something. I stood on that corner day after day with all the kids, and nobody talked to me. I made believe I was interested in looking at the trees and houses and clouds and stray dogs and whatever—anything not to let on how lonesome I felt inside. Many of the houses were interesting as far as middle-class neighborhoods go. In fact, I suppose you'd say it was a multi-class neighborhood because both the houses and the kids ranged from wrecks to rich. There'd be a lovely brick home with a lot of land, and right next to it there'd be a plain wooden house with a postage-stamp-sized lawn that needed cutting. The only thing that was completely high class was the trees. Large old trees lined most of the streets and had grown so tall and wide they almost touched. I loved looking at the trees more than anything at first, but after awhile even those started to depress me.

Then there was John.

I noticed him the very first day mainly because of his eyes. As I told you, he has these fantastic eyes that take in everything that's going on, and whenever they came my way, I looked in the other direction. His eyes reminded me of a description of a gigantic Egyptian eye that was found in one of the pyramids I read about in a book on black magic. Somehow an archaeologist's wife ended up with this huge stone eye in her bedroom, and in the middle of the night it exploded and a big cat started biting the archaeologist's wife's neck. When she put the lights on, the cat was gone. Only the pieces of the eye were scattered all over the floor. That's what John's eyes remind me of. I knew even from the first moment I saw him he had to be something special.

Then one day John had to sit next to me on the bus because all the other seats were taken. He wasn't sitting there for more than two minutes before he started laughing. Laughing right out loud, but not *to* anyone. I was so embarrassed I wanted to cry because I thought for sure he was laughing at me, and I turned my head all the way so the only thing I could see out the window of the bus was telephone poles going by. They call that paranoia. I knew that because some magazine did a whole article on mental disturbances, and after I read the symptoms of each of them, I realized I had all of them—but most of all I had paranoia. That's when you think everybody's making fun of you when they're not. Some extremely advanced paranoiacs can't even watch television because they think the canned laughter is about them. Freud would probably say it started with my mother picking on how I look all the time. But no matter how it started, I've got to admit that when anyone looks at me I'm sure they're noticing how awful my hair is or I'm too fat or my dress is funny. So I did think John was laughing at me, and it made me feel terrible, until finally—and the psychiatrists would say this was healthy—I began to get mad!

"Would you mind not laughing," I said, "because people think I'm sitting with a lunatic." He jumped when I spoke to him, so I realized he wasn't laughing at me. I don't think he even knew I was there.

"I'm sorry," he said. I just turned my head away and watched the telephone poles some more. Then I heard him whisper something under his breath, and it had just the tone of a first-class smart aleck.

"I am a lunatic."

I made believe I didn't hear it, but then he said it again a little louder.

"I *am* a lunatic."

"Well, I wouldn't go around bragging about it," I said, and I was so nervous I dropped one of my books on the floor. I was mortified picking it up because it fell between the seat and the window, and I was sure I'd look like an enormous cow bending over to get it. All I could think of at that moment was wishing one of his eyeballs would explode and a nice big cat would get at *his* neck, but I managed to get the book and sit straight up with this real annoyed look on my face.

Then he started that laughing again. Very quietly at first, and boy, did it burn me! And then I decided I was going to let out a little laugh, so I did. Then he laughed a little louder, and I laughed a little louder, and before I knew what was happening I couldn't stand it, so I really started laughing, and he started laughing, and we laughed so much the whole bus thought we were out of our minds.

3

Like Lorraine told you, I really am very handsome and do have fabulous eyes. But that doesn't get me much, except perhaps with Miss King, this English teacher I'm going to tell you about. I think she really goes for me the way she always laughs a little when she talks to me and says I'm such a card. A card she calls me, which sounds ridiculous coming out of the mouth of an old-maid English teacher who's practically fifty years old. I really hate it when a teacher has to show that she isn't behind the times by using some expression which sounds so up-to-date you know for sure she's behind the times. Besides, card really isn't up-to-date anymore, which makes it even more annoying. In fact, the thing Lorraine and I liked best about the Pigman was that he didn't go around saying we were cards or jazzy or cool or hip. He said we were delightful, and if there's one way to show how much you're not trying to make believe you're not behind the times, it's to go around saying people are delightful.

I had forgotten that stuff about paranoia in that magazine Lorraine gave me to read about seven months ago. She's always reading about eyes exploding and nutty people and beehives and things. The only part that impressed me out of the whole article was about the crazy lady in the sanitarium who hoarded food and sheets and towels and bathrobes—the one that used to wear all the bathrobes at one time. They said at one point she had hoarded 39 sheets, 42 towels, 93 English muffins—and she was wearing 8 bathrobes. Her big problem was she didn't feel secure. So they let her pick out as much as she wanted, and she ended up with 320 towels, 2,633 sheets, and 9,000 English muffins. Nine thousand English muffins!

But that's how it always is. Lorraine remembers the big words, and I remember the action. Which sort of makes sense when you stop to think that Lorraine is going to be a famous writer and I'm going to be a great actor. Lorraine thinks she could be an actress, but I keep telling her she'd have to be a character actress, which means playing washwomen on TV detective shows all the time. And I don't mean that as a distortion, like she always says I do. If anyone distorts, it's that mother of hers. The way her old lady talks you'd think Lorraine needed internal plastic surgery and seventeen body braces, but if you ask me, all she needs is a little confidence. She's got very interesting green eyes that scan like nervous radar—that is they used to until the Pigman died. Ever since then her eyes have become absolutely still, except when we work on this memorial epic. Her eyes come to life the second we talk about it. Her wanting to be a writer is part of it, I guess, but I think we're both a little anxious to get all that happened in place and try to understand why we did the crazy things we did.

I suppose it all started when Lorraine and I and these two amoebae called Dennis Kobin and Norton

Kelly were hot on these phone gags last September. We did the usual ones like dialing any number out of the book and asking "Is your refrigerator running?"

"Yes."

"Go catch it then."

And we called every drugstore.

"Do you have Prince Albert in a can?"

"Yes."

"Then let him out."

But then we made up a new game in which the object was to keep a stranger talking on the phone as long as possible. At least twice a week we'd meet for a telephone marathon. Wednesday afternoons we'd have it at Dennis' house because his mother goes shopping at the supermarket and his father doesn't get home from work until after six P.M., even when he's sober. And on Sundays we'd do it at Norton's because his father plays golf and his mother is so retarded she doesn't know what's coming off anyway, but at least they didn't mind if their kids used the house. Mine and Lorraine's we can't even go to. We couldn't use the phone at Lorraine's anyway because her mother doesn't have unlimited service, and at my house my mother is a disinfectant fanatic. She would have gotten too nervous over all of us using her purified instrument. Another difficulty there is that my father, whom I warmly refer to as Bore, put a lock on our phone—one of those round locks you put in the first dialhole so you can't dial. He put it on because of a little exchange we had when he called from work.

"Do you realize I've been trying to get your mother for an hour and a half and the line's been busy?" Bore bellowed.

"Those things happen. I was talking to a friend."

"If you don't use the phone properly, I'm going to put a lock on it."

"Yeah? No kidding?"

Now it was just the way I said *yeah* that set him off, and that night when he got home, he just put the lock on the phone and didn't say a word. But I'm used to it. Bore and I have been having a lot of trouble communicating lately as it is, and sometimes I go a little crazy when I feel I'm being picked on or not being trusted. That's why I finally put airplane glue in the keyhole of the lock so nobody could use the telephone, key or no key.

Anyway, the idea of the telephone marathon was you had to close your eyes and stick your finger on a number in the directory and then call it up to see how long you could keep whoever answered talking on the phone. I wasn't too good at this because I used to burst out laughing. The only thing I could do that kept them talking awhile before they hung up was to tell them I was calling from *TV Quiz* and that they had won a prize. That was always good for three and a half minutes before they caught on.

The longest anyone ever lasted was Dennis, because he picked out this old woman who lived alone and was desperate to talk to anyone. Dennis is really not very bright. In fact, he talks so slowly some people think he has brain damage. But he told this woman he had called her number because he had heard she gave good advice and his problem was that he was about to die from a hideous skin disease because a rat had bitten off his nose when he was a baby and the skin grafts didn't take. He kept her on the phone for two hours and twenty-six minutes. That was the record!

Now Lorraine can blame all the other things on

me, but she was the one who picked out the Pigman's phone number. If you ask me, I think he would have died anyway. Maybe we speeded things up a little, but you really can't say we murdered him.

Not murdered him.

4

John told you about Dennis and Norton, but I don't think he got across how really disturbed those two boys are. Norton has eyes like a mean mouse, and he's the type of kid who thinks everyone's trying to throw rusty beer cans at him. And he's pretty big, even bigger than John, and the two of them hate each other.

Actually, Norton is a social outcast. He's been a social outcast since his freshman year in high school when he got caught stealing a bag of marshmallows from the supermarket. He never recovered from that because they put his name in the newspaper and mentioned that the entire loot was a bag of marshmallows, and ever since then everybody calls him The Marshmallow Kid.

"How's The Marshmallow Kid today?"

Anyway, he's the one who started cheating in the telephone marathons we were having. After Dennis had rung up that staggering record about having his nose bitten off, Norton started getting smart, and when it was his turn to pick out a phone number, he'd peek a little and try to make his finger land on a woman's number rather than a man's. You could always make a woman talk twice as long as a man.

I used to ignore it because in his case it didn't matter whom he spoke to on the phone. They all hung up.

But this one time I decided to peek myself. When it was my turn, I made believe I had covered my eyes with my left hand, then thumbed through the pages, and as I moved my finger down a column I happened to spot the words "Howard Avenue." Now, Howard Avenue is just a few blocks from where I live, so I could pretend I belonged to the Howard Avenue Civic League or some other fictitious philanthropy.

There it was:

  Pignati Angelo 190 Howard Av YU1-6994

When this man answered, my voice was rather quivery because John was watching with his X-ray eyes and I think he knew I had cheated a bit. When he is an actor, I know he'll be able to project those glaring eyes clear up to the second balcony.

"Hello," this jolly voice said as I cleared my throat.

"Hello. Is this Mr. Angelo Pignati?"

"It sure is," came the bubbling voice again.

"This is Miss Truman of the Howard Avenue Charities. Perhaps you've heard of us and our good work?"

"My wife isn't home just now."

"I didn't call to speak with your wife, Mr. Pignati," I assured him. I changed to a very British accent. "I distinctly called to speak to you and summon you to our cause. You see, my organization is interested in receiving small donations from people just like you—good-hearted people, Mr. Pignati—we depend on lovely people just like you and your wife—"

"What did you say the name of your charity was?" the voice asked.

Suddenly I couldn't control myself anymore, and I burst into laughter right into the phone.

"Is something funny?"

"No . . . there's nothing funny, Mr. Pignati . . . it's just that one of the girls . . . here at the office has just told me a joke, and it was very funny." I bit my tongue. "But back to serious business, Mr. Pignati. You asked the name of our charity—the name of it is—"

"The Lorraine and John Fund!"

"The name of it is—"

"The Lorraine and John Fund," John repeated.

"Shut up," I said, covering the mouthpiece and then uncovering it. "The name of our charity is the L & J Fund, Mr. Pignati, and we'd like to know if you'd care to contribute to it? It would really be a very nice gesture, Mr. Pignati."

There was a pause.

"What was the joke the girl told you?" he finally said. "I know a lot of jokes, but my wife's the only one who laughs at them. Ha, ha."

"Is that so?"

"She really did laugh at them. She liked a good joke, she did, and I miss her. She's taken a little trip."

"Oh, did she?"

"Yep. She's out in California with my sister."

"Isn't that marvelous!"

"Her favorite was the one about the best get-well cards to get. Did you ever hear that one—what'd you say your name was?"

"Miss Truman."

"Well, Miss Truman, did you ever hear that one,

the one about what the best get-well cards you can get are?"

"No, Mr. Pignati—"

"It was my wife's favorite joke, that one was. She'd make me tell it a lot of times. . . ."

There was something about his voice that made me feel sorry for him, and I began to wish I had never bothered him. He just went on talking and talking, and the receiver started to hurt my ear. By this time Dennis and Norton had gone into the living room and started to watch TV, but right where they could keep an eye on timing the phone call. John stayed next to me, pushing his ear close to the receiver every once in awhile, and I could see the wheels in his head spinning.

"Yes, Miss Truman, the best get-well cards to get are four aces! Ha, ha, ha! Isn't that funny?"

He let out this wild laugh, as though he hadn't known the end of his own joke.

"Do you get it, Miss Truman? Four aces . . . the best get-well cards you can get—"

"Yes, Mr. Pignati—"

"You know, in *poker?*"

"Yes, Mr. Pignati."

He sounded like such a nice old man, but terribly lonely. He was just dying to talk. When he started another joke I looked at John's face and began to realize it was he who had started me telling all these prevarications.

John has made an art out of it. He prevaricates just for prevaricating's sake. It's what they call a compensation syndrome. His own life is so boring when measured against his daydreams that he can't stand it, so he makes up things to pretend it's exciting. Of course, when he gets caught in a lie, then he makes believe he was only telling the lie to make fun of whomever he was telling it to, but I think there's more to it than meets the eye. He can get so involved in a fib that you can tell he believes it enough to enjoy it. Maybe that's how all actors start. I don't know.

One time last term Miss King asked him what happened to the book report he was supposed to hand in on *Johnny Tremain*, and he told her that he had spilled some coffee on it the night before, and when the coffee dried, there was still sugar on the paper and so cockroaches ate the book report. You might also be interested in knowing that the only part of *Johnny Tremain* that John did end up reading was page forty-three—where the poor guy spills the molten metal on his hand and cripples it for life. That was the part he finally did his book report on— just page forty-three—and he got a ninety on it! I only got eighty-five, and I read the whole thing. Of course, writing book reports is not exactly the kind of writing I want to do. I don't want to report. I want to make things up. In a way I guess that's lying too, except I think you can tell the real truth with that kind of lying.

And John lies to his mother and father. He told them one time that he was hearing voices from outer space, and he thought creatures were going to come for him some night, so if they heard any strange noises coming from his room would they please call the police.

"Don't be silly," his mother told him and laughed it off with just the slightest bit of discomfort. His parents don't know quite what to make of him because neither of them has the imagination he has, and in a way they sort of respect it. Actually, I think they're a little frightened of it. But they're just as bad as he is when it comes to lying, and that may be the real reason they can't help John the way they should. From what I've seen of them, they don't seem to know what's true and what isn't true anymore. His father goes around bragging how he phonied up a car-insurance claim to get a hundred dollars to replace a piece of aluminum on their new car, which he had really replaced himself. Mrs. Conlan goes to the store and tells the clerk he forgot to give her Green Stamps the last time she was in, and she knows very well she's lying. It's a kind of subconscious, schizophrenic fibbing, if you ask me, and if those parents don't have guilt complexes, I don't know who has. I only hope I won't be that kind of adult.

"I don't know where you get that from, John!"

I do.

"Miss Truman, are you still there?"

"Yes, Mr. Pignati," I muttered.

"Well, did you get that joke? I didn't hear you laugh."

"No, I'm sorry I didn't get that joke."

"I didn't think you did. I said, 'In many states a hunting license entitles you to one deer and no more. Just like a marriage license.' Ha, ha, ha!"

"That's very funny, Mr. Pignati. That *is* very funny."

I must have sounded uncomfortable because he said, "I'm sorry if I'm taking up too much of your time, Miss Truman. You wanted a donation, did you say—for what charity?"

"The L & J Fund, Mr. Pignati." I bit my lip.

"I'll be glad to send you ten dollars, Miss Truman. Where do I send it?"

John bolted upright from his ridiculous position of pressing an ear against the receiver.

"Tell him to send it to your house."

"I will not!"

"Let me talk to him," John demanded, taking the phone right out of my hand. Just from the look in his eyes I knew what was going to happen. You just have to know how John does things, and you'll know one thing will always happen. He'll end up complicating everything.

5

You have to know how demented Dennis and Norton are to understand that when I told them Angelo Pignati caught on Lorraine was a phony and hung up, they believed it. I could tell them I went alligator hunting in St. Patrick's Cathedral last night, and they'd believe it. I just didn't want them to know Mr. Pignati had invited us over to his house the next day to give us the ten bucks for the L & J Fund. Especially Norton. If he knew about it, he'd try to hustle in on the deal, and he'd never stop at ten dollars. I didn't want anyone really to take advantage of the old man. Some people might think that's what I was doing, but not the way Norton would have. In fact, if Lorraine felt like saying one of us murdered Mr. Pignati, she should have blamed Norton. He's the one who finally caused all the trouble.

The next day Lorraine chickened out and said she wouldn't go with me to collect the money.

"Give me one good reason," I demanded.

"Because it's wrong to take money from an old man, that's why."

"All through history artists have survived by taking

money from old men. There's nothing wrong with having a patron."

"I don't want to talk about it."

"Don't you know anything?"

"I said I don't—"

"We can tell him the L & J Fund is intended to subsidize writers and actors if you want."

"You're crazy."

I decided not to push the matter, but I did need a dollar and a quarter for a six-pack, so when I got home I asked my Old Lady for it.

"No, no, no," she said in her best grating voice, all the while shining the coffee table in our sparkling living room, which sparkles because nobody's allowed to live in it. She's got plastic covers on everything. I mean, I like my Mom and all that, but she runs around like a chicken with its head cut off.

"Your father says you're not to have another penny until he speaks to you!"

"What did I do now?"

"You know very well what you did."

"No, I don't."

"Well, you just ask your father."

"I'm not asking him, I'm asking you."

"Kenneth never gave us any trouble," she just had to add, neatly folding the polishing rag.

"You just never caught him."

Kenneth is my older brother who's married and carries an attaché case to Wall Street every day. He's eleven years older than me.

"Get yourself a glass of milk, but rinse out the glass," she babbled, darting up the stairs. I could tell she just got back from the beauty parlor because her hair

was frizzed like she had just rammed her fingers into
an electric socket.

"What did I do?" I yelled from the kitchen as I
opened a Pepsi. Whenever she tells me to get a glass
of milk, I feel like a Pepsi and vice versa.

"What did I do?"

"You know!"

"*Please* tell me."

She came to the top of the stairs with a bottle of
hair spray in her hand. "You put glue in the telephone lock!" she wailed.

"I did *what?*"

"You heard me."

"I put glue in the telephone lock? Are you crazy?"

"When your father comes home we'll see who's
crazy." She gave her hair a quick spray to make sure
none of the frizz would disappear.

"I'm innocent."

"It was a very mean thing to do. Your father tried
to call his office this morning, and he couldn't get the
lock off. He couldn't dial!"

"I didn't do it."

"Then who did?"

"The ghost of Aunt Ahra."

"Your father'll have to talk to you," she said and
ran upstairs. Then I heard her vacuuming in her bedroom.

I blame an awful lot of things on the ghost of Aunt
Ahra because she died in our house when she was
eighty-two years old. She was really my father's
mother's sister, if you can figure that one out, and
she had lived with us ever since the time she took a
hot bath in her own apartment and couldn't get out
of the bathtub for three days. They found her when

she finally managed to throw a bottle of shampoo through the bathroom window, and it splattered all over the side of a neighbor's house. The neighbor thought it was the work of a juvenile delinquent at first, which is sort of funny if you think about it awhile.

"So you're not going to give me a dollar twenty-five; is that what you're trying to communicate to me?"

"He couldn't even dial his own office."

"I told you the ghost of Aunt Ahra did it."

"This is not a joking matter."

"Mother, your hypertension is showing."

Well, that severed maternal relations for the afternoon, and I had no intention of waiting for Bore to come home. I decided to give Lorraine the signal to meet me, so I picked up the phone and tapped the connection button ten times, which is the same as dialing O. The keyhole of the lock was still expertly crammed with glue.

"Yes?"

"Hello, operator? Would you please get me Yul-1219?"

"You can dial that number yourself, sir."

"No, I can't. You see, operator, I have no arms."

"I'm sorry, sir."

"They've got this phone strapped to my head for emergency calls, so I'd appreciate it if you'd connect me."

"I'll be happy to, sir."

As soon as I could hear the number ring once I hung up. That was always the signal for Lorraine to meet me at the corner of Eddy and Victory Boulevard if she could get out of the house.

"You're ruining your lungs with that thing" was the first remark out of her mouth besides a cough from a misdirected puff from my cigarette. She sounds just like her mother when she says that.

"I've been thinking, and I've decided we'd better go over and collect the ten bucks."

"I've been thinking, and I've decided we'd definitely better not," she snapped.

"We're not doing anything bad," I insisted.

"Ha!"

"He sounded lonely on the phone, now didn't he?"

"So what?"

"Lonely people need visitors, so. . . ." I made believe I wanted to look at a new Chevy going by so she couldn't see my eyes. "So it's our duty to visit the lonely."

"You never wanted to visit lonely people before, or is it that you only like lonely people who have ten dollars?"

"You think you're the perfect headshrinker with all those psychology books you read, and you really don't know a thing."

She sat down on the bus-stop bench, and I could see her biting her lip. She does that every once in awhile when she doesn't know what to say. That's when I know all I have to do is push her a little further and I'll get what I want.

"You read all those books, and you don't even know when a man is thinking about committing suicide."

"Stop it, John."

"You think I'm kidding?"

"He did not sound like he was thinking of suicide."

"You only know about the obvious kind—like when someone's so desperate they're going to jump off a bridge or slit their wrists. There are other kinds, you know."

"Like what?"

"Like the subconscious kind. You're always blabbing about the subconscious, and you can't even tell a subconscious suicide when you talke to one."

She started biting her lip again.

"He sounded just like the kind of guy who'd commit suicide by taking a cold shower and then leaving the windows open to die of pneumonia!"

That made her burst out laughing, and then I knew I had her where I wanted her.

"Just think of all the joy we can bring into his life."

One-ninety Howard Avenue turned out to be just across the street from a big convent, and there were a lot of trees and stuff and nuns running around the place. There were a lot of nice houses on the street too, but one-ninety was a phenomenal dump.

As soon as she saw the house Lorraine stopped.

"Maybe he's poor," she said. "Look at this place."

I figured he must have enough money if he offered it over the phone like that without even knowing what our charity did. A couple of nuns were strolling on the lawn of the convent and staring at us kind of funny.

"Or he could be a sex maniac," Lorraine threw in for good measure. That's her mother again.

"Wishful thinking," I said, and Lorraine couldn't help laughing. And while she was laughing I rang the bell.

When Angelo Pignati came to the door, I wish you could have seen him. He was in his late fifties and was pretty big, and he had a bit of a beer stomach.

But the part that slaughtered me was this great big smile on his face. He looked so glad to see us I thought his eyes were going to twinkle out of his head. He would've made one @#$% of a Santa Claus if you had put a white beard on him and stuck him on a street corner in December with a little whiskey on his breath.

"Hi! Are you the charity people?" He didn't seem to be surprised that we were kids. He just seemed glad to see us.

"Yes. This is Miss Truman, and I am Mr. Wander-meyer."

The house had a nice warm smell to it. We had to walk through a hall that had a lot of old junk stored in it, and then we went into this living room that had all that old kind of stuffed furniture with lace things that cover the arms so you don't wear them out.

"Please sit down," he said, smiling away like crazy. "I've got some good homemade wine, if you like."

"That'll be just fine, don't you think, Miss Truman?"

"Yes ... yes."

Well, actually I might as well tell you we were both scared stiff when he went into the kitchen. At first he seemed too nice to be for real, but when I looked at Lorraine and she looked at me, I could tell we both were thinking what we'd do if Mr. Pignati came prancing out of the kitchen with a big knife in his hand. He could've been some psycho with an electric carving knife who'd dismember our bodies and wouldn't get caught until our teeth clogged up the sewer or something like that. I mean, I thought of all those things, and I figured if he did come running out with a knife, I'd grab hold of the ugly table lamp right next to me and bop him one on the skull. I mean, if you're going to survive nowadays, you really have to think a bit ahead.

He returned with three glasses of wine and that enormous smile of his.

Poison perhaps.

"I just got back from the zoo," he said, sitting in this armchair that seemed to swallow him up. I could see Lorraine looking all around, checking the dust in the corners and the pieces of electrical equipment that were scattered on one table. "I take a walk over to the zoo every day. My wife usually goes with me, but she's in California visiting my sister."

"Really?" Lorraine said, taking a sip of the dark wine.

"That's why the place is such a mess," he added, pointing to the electrical junk. "When she's home, she makes me put all that away. I'm a retired electrician, you know."

"How long has she been gone?" Lorraine asked, trying to be kind, in that English accent of hers.

"She's been out there about a month now."

For a moment he looked as though he was going to cry, and then suddenly he changed the subject. Lorraine's nervous radar was in full operation, and I could tell it made her sad to look at the old man.

"While I was waiting for you I was practicing how to memorize ten items. Do you know the secret of how to memorize ten items?"

I looked at him, and I had to bite my tongue because I was going to burst out laughing. He looked just like a great big kid—so happy we were there.

"You just mention ten objects, and I'll memorize

them right off the bat. You give me one, Miss Truman, and then you give me one, Mr.—?"

"Wandermeyer," I offered, with just the right touch of disdain I thought.

"I'm afraid I don't understand you, Mr. Pignati," Lorraine said.

"Just give me an object. Just say any object. Go on."

"Girl?" Lorraine said, her accent getting a little shaky.

"Now you give me one," he said excitedly, pointing at me. "And here's a piece of paper and a pencil to write the words down. Just don't let me see them."

"Couch," I said.

"Boy," Lorraine went on.

"Eye."

"Chair."

"Dog."

"Bird."

"Stop sign."

"Lighthouse."

"Cockroach."

Mr. Pignati sat forward in the seat, beaming. "Now I'm going to repeat them back to you. Did you write them all down so you can check me? Did you get them all down?"

"Yes, Mr. Pignati."

He started. "Cockroach, lighthouse, stop sign, bird, dog, chair, eye, boy, couch, girl. Is that right? Was I right?"

"Yes, Mr. Pignati."

Then he said the items, starting with girl and working back to cockroach, and I swear he looked just like a great big baby that had just made a superduper

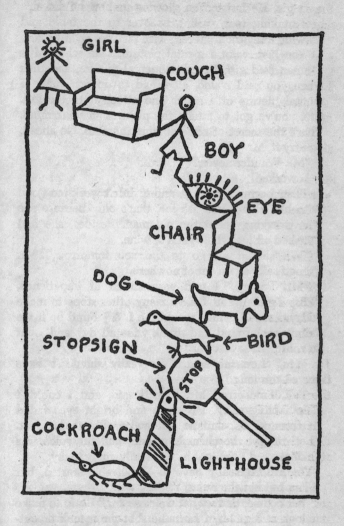

mud pie. He insisted on showing us how he did this breathtaking feat, calling us over to the table and drawing a diagram.

"You just make a mental picture. Like when Miss Truman said *girl*, I made a mental picture, and then when you said *couch*, all I had to do was make a mental picture of a couch and attach it to the girl. See, you've got to attach the pictures in your mind. That's the secret of remembering them all. Go ahead, you try it, Mr.—?"

"Mr. Wandermeyer."

It worked!

Then Lorraine tried it, and it didn't work too good with her. But if you ask me, that's only because she was worrying about the old man. Besides, she had polished off her whole glass of wine.

"We should all go to the zoo tomorrow," Mr. Pignati said, again out of nowhere.

"Mr. Pignati," I said with an air of impatience, "Miss Truman and I have many other stops to make today. I mean, where would the L & J Fund be if we simply sat around and drank wine all day and went to zoos?"

"Yes," Lorraine said. "We really shouldn't have stayed this long."

"Oh, I'm sorry," Mr. Pignati said, and I couldn't help feeling sorry. His smile and bright eyes faded in front of us, and he got awkwardly to his feet. "Let me get the check," he said, and his voice was so depressed I thought he was really going to cry.

"You don't really have to—" Lorraine started, but he looked bewildered.

"Of course, that's what we came for," I said to make it look real at least. Lorraine shot me a look of outrage.

"Of course," he said.

We watched him go down another hall to a room that had black curtains on the doorway. I mean, there was no door, just these curtains. He disappeared through them. When he finally came back out, he seemed to be very tired, and he started writing the check.

"Whom should I make it out to?" he asked.

Lorraine gulped and went speechless.

"Cash will be fine. Make it out to cash," I found myself saying.

He handed me the check, and my hand shook a little. It wasn't that I was scared or anything, but it was an awful lot of money.

"On behalf of the L & J Fund I accept this check."

"Oh, *yes*," Lorraine echoed, and I could tell she was furious with me because her eyes were starting to flit all over the place again.

"Do you think you might like to go to the zoo with me *someday?*" Mr. Pignati asked just as I knew Lorraine was getting ready to flee out of the house.

"I always go to the zoo." The old man laughed. "I love animals. My wife and I both love animals, but . . . I've been going to the zoo by myself lately. I always go. Every day."

"You love animals . . . ?" Lorraine muttered, her left hand opening the front door just a crack.

There was a dreadful pause.

"Oh, I forgot to show you my pigs!" he exclaimed, the gleam returning to his eyes. "You didn't see my pigs, did you?"

There came another terrible pause.

"No . . . we didn't see . . . your pigs," I said.

He gestured us back into the living room and then moved down the hall to the room at the far end—

the one with the black curtains hanging on the side
of the entrance. Lorraine didn't want to follow him,
but I dragged her behind me until we got to the
doorway.

"Ohh-h-h!" Lorraine stammered.

The room was dark because its two windows were
covered with faded paper shades. It was a real
dump except for the table and shelves at the far end
of it. The table had pigs all over it. And the shelves
had pigs all over them. There were pigs all over the
place. It was ridiculous. I never saw so many pigs.
I don't mean the live kind; these were phony pigs.
There were glass pigs and clay pigs and marble
pigs.

Lorraine reached her hand out.

"Touch them," he told her. "Don't be afraid to pick
them up." It was a big change from my mother who
always lets out a screech if you go near anything, so
I couldn't help liking this old guy even if he was
sort of weird.

There were pigs that had *Made in Japan* on them.
Some were from Germany and Austria and Switzer-
land. There were pigs from Russia and lots of pigs
from Italy, naturally. There were little pigs and big
pigs. Ugly ones and cute ones. There were blue,
black, yellow, orange, striped, green, and rainbow-
colored pigs. Pigs, pigs, pigs!

"Don't you like them?" he asked.

"Oh, everybody loves pigs," I said.

"My wife collects pigs. I got her started on it when
I gave her one to remind her of me—before we got
married."

"Oh?"

"This one," he said, lifting a large white pig with

an ugly smile on its face, "this one was the first one I got her. She thought it was very funny. Pig. *Pig-*nati. Do you get it?"

"Yes, Mr. Pignati. We get it."

6

Right after we left the Pigman's, John dragged me down to Tony's Market, which is on the corner of Victory Boulevard and Cebra Avenue. All the kids go to Tony's because he sells beer to anyone and for some reason the police leave him alone. John thinks he pays them off, but I think it's just that old Tony has a nice, friendly face and believes in the old days when they thought a little alcohol was good for everyone. He's sort of a father-image with a cultural lag.

"You're not going to cash that check," I said. "You can send it back to him in an envelope or tear it up or—"

"If we don't cash it, he'll know something was funny and really call the police," he told me with typical John Conlan logic.

"Who are you kidding?"

"I mean it. *Really.*"

I refused to talk to him for five minutes while I drank a chocolate drink I bought with my own money while John cashed the check and got a six-pack of beer and a pack of cigarettes. I just stared at him drinking his beer and waited to see how long it would take for him to feel guilty.

"Wouldn't you love to go to the zoo?"

"No."

"Don't be a killjoy."

"Why should we go to the zoo? Do you mind telling me that?"

"What do you mean *why?*" He raised his voice, which is typical when he needs to delay a second because he's at a loss for his next distortion. "We owe him something after taking ten dollars from him, don't we?"

"What did you take the money for in the first place?" I practically screamed.

John jumped at my outburst and then slowly sipped his beer. He smiled and said sweetly, "You're a little schizo today, aren't you?"

I didn't get home that night until after six thirty, and I was a little scared when I found my mother there. She's a private nurse and was supposed to be working a four-to-twelve shift that night. I never have to worry about finding my father there because he left fifteen years ago when they got a legal separation, and then he died six years ago, which made it a more permanent separation. As it is, my mother's enough to worry about.

"Where were you?"

"I went to a drama-club meeting."

"Until now?" She fumbled with the buttons of her white uniform, which gave me a moment to think.

"I had a soda with the kids afterwards at Stryker's Luncheonette."

"I don't want you going in there. I told you that."

"All the kids go there."

"I don't care what all the kids do. I don't want you in there. I've seen those boys hanging around there, and they've only got one thing on their minds."

My mother's got a real hang-up about men and boys.

"You didn't tell me about it yesterday." She put her faded blue bathrobe over her slip. "My legs hurt."

"I'm sorry."

"The old fossil had me on the run from the minute I got there." She started brushing her hair. "At least his worries are over."

"Did he die?"

"Of course he died. I told his daughter two days ago he wasn't going to last the week. Put some coffee water on."

I was glad to be able to get out to the kitchen because it makes me sad to watch my mother brush her hair. My mom is a very pretty woman when she has her long brown hair down, and when she smiles, which is hardly ever. She just doesn't look the way she sounds, and I often wonder how she got this way. It's not exactly easy being her daughter, and more than once I've thought about what a good psychiatrist could do for her. Actually, I think her problems are so deep-rooted she'd need three years of intensive psychoanalysis.

"I mean the old guy's throat was closing, and he was bouncing up and down in bed for days. If they don't think I know when a cancer patient is going to wind up, they're very much mistaken."

"Yes, Mother."

"I don't feel like eating anything. I had a few pieces of roast beef out of their refrigerator, and I brought home some canned goods I borrowed from the pantry. They'll never miss them. The family has started fighting over his money already. I think there's a can of turkey soup. Why don't you have that?"

I can't tell you what she'd do if *I* ever took anything, but she isn't even ashamed of what she does. She figures they don't pay her enough, so she'll even it up her own way.

She came into the kitchen and opened a jar of instant coffee. I handed her this oversized coffee cup I gave her for her last birthday. It has "MOM" painted in huge letters on one side. She cried when she unwrapped it.

"Here's two dollars for your sophomore dues," she said, putting the money down on the table. "That school thinks it's easy for a woman to support a kid by herself—two dollars for this, five dollars for that . . . twenty-three bucks for a dental certificate! I can't even afford to get myself a pair of nylons." She pulled her bathrobe up and moved so quickly toward me I thought she was going to hit me. "Look at them! There're so many runs you'd think a cat chewed them."

"I could wait another week to pay the dues."

"Pay it now. Nobody is going to talk about us behind our backs. Besides, I got an extra ten from Solvies."

"What?"

"Solvies the undertaker. The family let me call Solvies, and they always slip me an extra ten for the business. How's the turkey soup?"

"Fine."

"I heard Berdeen's Funeral Parlor is slipping twenty under the table, so maybe I'll give them a little business when the next one croaks. As soon as this one died I called the Nurses' Registry, but they won't have anything for me until the day after tomorrow. Another terminal cancer." She sat down opposite me at the table and lifted the cup to her lips. I tried to keep my eyes on the big painted letters.

"I think it'd be a good idea if you stayed home from school and cleaned the house with me tomorrow."

"I have a Latin test."

"Can't you make it up?"

"No," I said quietly, hoping she wouldn't explode. Sometimes it's just the way I say one word that gets her going, and she's so quick with her hand it's hard to think of her being gentle to sick people.

"I can't go out and earn a living and keep this house decent. You've got to do something."

I blew on a spoonful of soup. "I did the laundry yesterday."

"It's about time."

"And I changed the sheets on the bed."

"You sleep in it too, you know." I was sorry I had said anything.

"Look up the telephone number of Berdeen's Funeral Parlor for me and jot it down. I want to have it handy just in case."

I put my soup spoon down.

"Are you sure you can't stay home tomorrow?"

"Yes."

"I think you could take a year off from that school and not miss anything."

"The test is very important."

"Yeah, it's important. Later on in life I'm sure you're going to run around talking Latin all over the place."

I've often wondered what she'd say if she knew I wanted to be a writer. Writer! I can just hear her.

After she went to bed, I called John. His mother

answered the phone, and I could tell there was some trouble over there.

"Do you still want to go to the zoo tomorrow?"

"Yeah."

"Well, it's all right with me," I whispered, keeping one eye on the bedroom door.

"What made you change your mind?"

"I just think I need a day off. What's all that yelling in the background?"

"It's just the Bore."

"What did you do now?"

He raised his voice. "They're trying to accuse me of gluing the telephone lock. They don't trust me around here."

"Lorraine!" The voice came from the bedroom. "Who are you talking to?"

"Jane Appling. I forgot what chapter the Latin test is going to cover."

"Hurry up and finish."

"Good-bye, Jane," I said into the phone.

The next day we cut school. That's easy because this girl by the name of Deanna Deas is in love with John and she happens to work in the Dean's office which gets the cut and absentee cards the teachers send down—if they happen to remember. So Deanna said she'd fix it up so John and I wouldn't get anything sent home, although I'll bet she was sorry she wasn't cutting with John. Somehow I don't really think she was jealous. People just don't get jealous of me. I'm the type the boss's wife would hire for her husband's secretary. Deanna Deas is the type the boss's wife would definitely not hire. She even bleaches her hair.

John had called the Pigman and made arrangements for us to meet him in front of the zoo at ten o'clock in the morning. We didn't want to be seen walking around our neighborhood with him, but the zoo was far enough away so we knew we'd be safe once we got there.

John and I arrived around nine thirty and sat down on the benches at the entrance. The sea-lion pool is right there, and that kept John busy while I was combing my hair and polishing my Ben Franklin sunglasses. I don't wear all crazy clothes, but I do like my Ben Franklin sunglasses because everyone looks at me when I wear them. I used to be afraid to have people look at me, but ever since I met John I seem to wear little things that make them look. He wears phony noses and moustaches and things like that. He's even got a big pin that says "MY, YOU'RE UGLY," and he wears that once in awhile.

I really didn't want to go to the zoo. I don't like seeing all those animals and birds and fish behind bars and glass just so a lot of people can stare at them. And I particularly hate the Baron Park Zoo because the attendants there are not intelligent. They really aren't. The thing that made me stop going to the zoo a few years ago was the way one attendant fed the sea lions. He climbed up on the big diving platform in the middle of the pool and unimaginatively just dropped the fish into the water. I mean, if you're going to feed sea lions, you're not supposed to plop the food into the tank. You can tell by the expressions on their faces that the sea lions are saying things like "Don't dump the fish in!"

"Pick the fish up one by one and throw them into the air so we can chase after them."

"Throw the fish in different parts of the tank!"

"Let's have fun!"

"Make a game out of it!"

If my mother had ever let me have a dog, I think it would have been the happiest dog on earth. I know just how the minds of animals work—just the kind of games they like to play. The closest I ever came to having a pet was an old mongrel that used to hang around the neighborhood. I thought there was nothing wrong with sitting on the front steps and petting him, but my mother called the ASPCA, and I know they killed him.

At ten o'clock sharp, Mr. Pignati arrived.

"Hi!" he said. His smile stretched clear across his face. "Hope I'm not late?"

"Right on time, Mr. Pignati. Right on time," John answered.

I felt sorry for the old man because people just don't go around smiling like that all the time unless they're mentally unbalanced or harboring extreme anxiety.

"What'll it be first? Peanuts? Soda? The Snake Building?" He sounded so excited you'd have thought we had just landed on Venus.

I should have just left there and then because I knew things were going to get involved. I realize now there were plenty of bad omens within the next few minutes. If I'd had half a brain, I'd have Pogo-sticked it right out of there.

The first was a woman selling peanuts. I went up to her and said, "I want four bags of peanuts."

"How many bags?" she said.

"Four bags."

"Well, why didn't you say so?"

I mean, that's how antagonistic she was. A real devoted antagonist. You could tell she hated kids— just hated them. I don't know whether one of the requirements of dealing with kids is that you have to hate them to begin with, or whether working with kids makes you hate them, but one way or another it works out that way—except with people like the Cricket, and she doesn't really know what we're like.

That was the first omen. I should have left right on the spot.

Then I was attacked by a peacock. This low-IQ peacock came tearing after me as soon as it heard me open my bag of peanuts. They let them run around loose at Baron Park Zoo, and this white one opened up all its feathers and started dancing in front of me and backing me up against a fence.

"Just offer it a peanut." The Pigman was grinning. "He likes you. Ha, ha."

The third omen that this was going to be a bad day was when we went into the nocturnal room of the Mammal Building. The whole room is pretty dark so you can see these animals that only come out at night, like owls and pottos and cute little vampire bats. I had never seen this nocturnal room before, and I almost went into shock when I got a look at the vampire bats. They had some explanatory pictures next to their glass cage that showed a couple of bats sucking the blood out of a horse's neck while the horse was sleeping.

But that wasn't the part that was the third omen. I mean, that exhibit would have been there on any day. It was this child that I thought was an omen— a little kid about ten years old who was sitting right up on the railing and leaning against the glass of the bat cage. Only he wasn't looking at the bats. He was looking at *you* when you came to look at the bats. And when I came up to the cage to see these ugly blood-sucking creatures, I had to look right into this little kid's face that had a smirk on it. He made me feel as though I was a bat in a cage and he was on the outside looking in at me. It all made me very nervous.

But Mr. Pignati just loved the nocturnal room, and the only one who loved it more was John. John likes things like king vultures and alligators. He was even excited in the snake house. As far as snakes go, I think once you've seen one, you've seen them all. So I let him and the Pigman go on running around while I took this snake quiz that was on a lighted sign. They had ten statements and you had to pick out which ones were false.

1. All poisonous snakes have triangular-shaped heads.

2. Some snakes have stingers in their tails.

3. You can tell a rattlesnake's age by the number of rattles it has.

4. Milk snakes will milk a farmer's cow.

5. Large snakes can live for more than a year without food.

6. Snakes cannot close their eyes.

7. Coachwhip snakes will whip people.

8. Some snakes can roll like a hoop to overtake their victim.

9. A horsehair rope will keep snakes away from a campfire.

10. Snakes can hypnotize their prey.

I mean, it was not exactly a depth quiz. I was right on every one of them. Just in case you're trying to take it, I won't put down which of the statements are false until the end of this chapter.

Anyway, after seeing Galapagos tortoises, reticulated pythons, and puff adders, the Pigman dragged us over to the Primate Building, more popularly known as the monkey house.

"I want you to meet Bobo."

"Bobo?" Even John's eyes widened.

"My best friend," Mr. Pignati explained.

We stopped in front of a cage with bars, only about three feet from where we stood. Let me tell you, Bobo could have used a good spray deodorant. A little door was open at the back of the cage, and apparently Bobo was in the inner part where they get fed.

"Bobo?" the Pigman called out sweetly.

John looked at me and I looked at him and he rolled his eyes up into his head.

"Bobo? Come out and say hello!"

At last Bobo decided to make an appearance. He was the ugliest, most vicious-looking baboon I've ever seen in my life. I mean a real baboon. And there's the Pigman, the smiling Pigman, leaning all the way over the guardrail, tossing peanuts to this mean baboon. Mr. Pignati would take a peanut, hold it up in the air, and say, "Bobo want a peanut?" And Bobo would show these monstrous teeth that looked like dentures when they don't quite fit, and the beast would grunt and swoon and move its head from side to side. "*Uggga. Ugggal*"

Mr. Pignati was throwing peanuts right and left. About every third one would hit the bars and fall where the baboon couldn't reach it. Sometimes Bobo would catch the peanut like a baseball. And the expressions on both their faces got to be upsetting. John had gotten bored with Bobo and moved down to the next cage that had a gorilla. He was imitating Tarzan and going *AaaaaaaayaaaaaaaaaH!*—which I don't think was the most original performance that gorilla had ever seen. Can you imagine what gorillas must think after being in a zoo a few years and hearing practically every boy who comes to look at them go *AaaaaaaayaaaaaaaaaH?* If that isn't enough to give an animal paranoia, I don't know what is.

It was obvious that Mr. Pignati was going to visit awhile with Bobo, and John and I felt like we were intruding.

"Miss Truman and I are going to get on the touring car," John finally announced.

"Yes. . . ." Mr. Pignati muttered, tossing another peanut to Bobo.

"Mr. Pignati, we'll meet you back here in twenty minutes." I wanted to make sure he understood.

"I'll be right here with Bobo—"

"I'm sure you will," John added as we went out of the monkey house and got on this mechanical contraption that came by. It looked like a train, and it had five cars with rubber wheels because it didn't run on a track. It only went about four miles an hour, and it's a good thing because this blond-haired boy driving the thing looked like he didn't quite know what he was doing.

I was getting full about this time because I had eaten more peanuts than Bobo, so I just sat back and watched the landscape drift by. We passed the bald eagle (which is also the nickname for the principal of our high school), the white-tailed deer, tahr goats, three white-bearded gnu, lions in a pit, one otter, a black leopard, a striped hyena ("a raider of graves"), two cheetahs that were fighting, four Bengal tigers, a Kodiak bear, an American bear, a polar bear, two hippos ("which secrete a fluid the color of blood all over their body"), an eight-ton bull elephant, and a giant anteater.

By that time we were almost back to the Primate Building, so we jumped off the tiny train and watched the alligators being fed. They were in a big outdoor pool, and two attendants were throwing huge chunks of meat and bone right at them. They ate the bones and all. It really made me feel like gagging. I mean, I just don't see any point in having animals like that running around on earth. I think God goofed in that department, if you ask me.

When we got back to Mr. Pignati, he had a fresh supply of peanuts and was still chucking them over to Bobo, who kept flashing his dentures at him. Then John decided to strike up a conversation with the gorilla. Only the gorilla started to make these terrifying noises, and John started to make believe *he* was a monkey and began screaming back at the gorilla. I joined in finally and got this pair of chimpanzees going. "*Uggauggaboo*" I told them, and they knew right away it was a game.

I thought Mr. Pignati was going to blow his top with all that nonsense going on because at first he just looked at us, and I don't mean with a smile.

Then I heard this "*Uggauggaboo*," and I'll be darned if it wasn't Mr. Pignati starting in. And before you knew it, all three of us were going *Uggauggaboo*, and we had Bobo, two chimps, and the gorilla worked up into such a tizzy I thought the roof of the monkey house was going to fall in.

"I'll miss you, Bobo," Mr. Pignati said as we were leaving.

And when Bobo realized he wasn't going to get any more peanuts, you should have seen the expression on his face!

P.S. *The answer to the snake quiz is that only statements five and six are true.*

7

I don't happen to buy all of Lorraine's stuff about omens. She talks about me distorting, but look at her. I mean, she thinks she can get away with her subliminal twists by calling them omens, but she doesn't fool me. The only difference between her fibs and mine are that hers are eerie—she's got a gift for saying things that make you anxious.

I happen to have enjoyed that little trip to the zoo even if she didn't. I think it was sort of nice that a baboon had a friend like Mr. Pignati. I'd say that baboon was @#$% lucky. As a matter of fact, the way the Pigman was treating Lorraine and me you'd have thought he liked us as much as Bobo. He bought me two cotton-candies-on-a-stick, one bag of peanuts, and a banana split at this homemade ice-cream palace. Lorraine got at least four bags of peanuts, one cherry ice-cream cone, and a black-and-white soda. If you let her, Lorraine would eat until she dropped, and if she keeps going at that rate, I'm afraid she's going to be somewhat more than voluptuous. She could end up just plain fat.

We finally told him to call us Lorraine and John because every time he'd say Mr. Wandermeyer I'd forget that was supposed to be me. Besides, he was harmless—a little crazy—but really harmless.

Lorraine and I went to school the following day, and we didn't get over to the Pigman's until that night around seven o'clock. That was because when we were heading over there at three thirty, we ran into Dennis and Norton who wanted to know where we were going. We made believe we weren't going anywhere, so we had to go to the cemetery to have a beer with them. We drink at a special part of the cemetery called Masterson's Tomb. That's where all the famous Mastersons are buried, you know. It's a fantastic place because they have acres and acres all for their own tomb, and it's fenced in with a private road which they only open up when one of the Mastersons dies. But there is a hole in the fence at one place in the woods, and that's where all the kids go through.

The tomb is a great big marble building that's set in the side of a hill so only the fancy front sticks out. The columns and everything are nice, but it's all chained up, so we climb up the side of the hill and get on top by these two glass domes that let you peek down inside. You can't actually see anything, but it sure makes you wonder.

I think cemeteries are one of the loveliest places to be—if you're not dead, of course. The hills and green grass and flowers are much nicer than what you get when you're alive. Sometimes we go there at midnight and hide behind stones to scare the @‡$% out of each other.

Once I ran away from Lorraine and the others and hid in a part of the cemetery that didn't have perpetual care. That's the part where no one pays to keep the grass cut. I was just lying on my back, looking up at the stars, and I was so loaded I thought I could feel the spin of the earth. All those stars millions of light years away shining down on me—me glued to a minor planet spinning around its own gigantic sun.

I stretched out and touched stone. I remember pulling my hands back to my sides, just keeping my eyes on the stars, concentrating on bringing them in and out of focus. "Is there anyone up there trying to talk to me? Anybody up there?"

"Anybody *down* there?" If I was lying on somebody's grave, whoever it was would be six feet away. Maybe there had been a lot of erosion, and whoever it was was only five feet away . . . or four. Maybe the tombstone had sunk at the same rate as the erosion, and the body was only a foot away below me—or an inch. Maybe if I put my hand through the grass, I would feel a finger sticking out of the dirt—or a hand. Perhaps both arms of a corpse were on either side of me right at that moment. What could be left? A few bones. The skull. The worms and bacteria had eaten the rest. Water in the earth had dissolved parts, and the plants had sucked them up. Maybe one of the molecules of iron from the corpse's hemoglobin is in the strand of grass next to my ear. But the imbalmers drain all the blood—well, probably not *every* drop. Nobody does anything perfectly.

Then I got very sad because I knew I wasn't really wondering about the guy underneath me, whoever he was. I was just interested in what was going to happen to me. I think that's probably the real reason I go to the graveyard. I'm not afraid of seeing ghosts.

I think I'm really *looking* for ghosts. I *want* to see them. I'm looking for anything to prove that when I drop dead there's a chance I'll be doing something a little more exciting than decaying.

Anyway, we finally got away from Norton and Dennis, but it was too late to go over to the Pigman's —mainly because Lorraine had to get home to check in with her mother.

She finally got out of the house again that night by performing an elaborate ritual about having to go to the library. As for myself, I didn't have much of a problem.

"Eat you peas, John," the Old Lady said, dabbing her mouth with a napkin. "Don't roll them around."

"I'm not rolling them around."

"Your mother said to stop it," Bore ordered. It was the first thing he'd said to me during dinner, and even though it wasn't the warmest remark, I could tell he had given up prosecuting the case of the phantom gluer.

"Your father sold over three hundred lots today," the Old Lady said, like she was patting a cocker spaniel on the head. Bore has a seat on the Coffee Exchange, and if he sells more than two hundred lots in a day, he's in a good mood. Anything less than that and there's trouble.

"It was like pulling teeth," Bore returned, slightly embarrassed but pleased with the praise. He cut deep into the steak on his plate. "Wait until you start working, John."

"I have to get the dessert," the Old Lady said, violently polishing a teaspoon and dashing out to the kitchen. She always gets terrified if it looks like my father and I are going to have any type of discussion. A suitable pause occurred after Hyper left the room, and then he started in.

"I think your problem is you have too much spare time."

"That's an interesting point of view."

"Don't be fresh. I was thinking maybe you'd like to work with me over at the Exchange a few days a week. Just after school?"

I almost choked on a mouthful of yams when he said that. I mean, I've been over to the Exchange and seen all the screaming and barking Bore has to do just to earn a few bucks, and if he thought I was going to have any part of that madhouse, he had another thought coming.

"It'd be better than the way you waste all your time now. After all, what are you going to do in life?"

"I'm thinking of becoming an actor."

"Don't be a jackass."

"You asked me what I'm going to do, and I told you."

"Your brother is doing very well at the Exchange. He makes a fine living, and there's still room for you. I've only got a few years left, and somebody has to take over."

"Kenny will."

"The business can be half yours, and you know it. I can't take the strain much longer."

Every time he says that, I get a little sick to my stomach because I know it's true. He's almost sixty years old, and I know he's not going to be around much longer. All the guys at the Exchange drop dead of heart attacks. They gather around this circle and bellow out bids all day long, like Mexicans at a bull-fight.

"Pass me the butter, please."

"Just a couple of hours a day. You could help me close out the accounts. Even a dummy can learn how to do that."

"Yes, I *could*—"

"An actor?" Bore blurted, as if it finally got through to him. "Thank God Kenneth isn't a lunatic."

"Dad, it's the only thing I'm really interested in doing. I want to go to acting school right after graduation. Everyone says that's what I should be, with my imagination—"

"Try eating your imagination when you're hungry sometime."

"I just don't want to wear a suit every day and carry an attaché case and ride a subway. I want to be *me*. Just me. Not a phony in the crowd."

"Who's asking you to be a phony?"

"You are."

"I'm asking you to try working for a change. At your age I was working hard, not floundering around in a fool's dream world."

"Do you both want whipped cream and nuts on your strawberry whirl?" The Old Lady stood at the kitchen door, wiping forks a mile a minute. I should have said nothing, but it was a conditioned reflex.

"Do you mean *real* whipped cream or that horrible, prepared-mix, fake whipped cream?"

"Don't give the ingrate anything."

"He's only joking."

The Hyper was off again.

There was a terrible pause.

"I apologize."

"One of these days it'll be too late to apologize. Your mother isn't going to be around forever either, you know. When she's dead, you're going to wish to God you'd been nicer to her. Mark my words." He sliced another piece of steak and groaned when the knife wouldn't go through a bit of gristle.

"Oh Dad, can't you see all I want to do is be individualistic?"

"Don't worry about that."

"I want to be *me*."

"Who's asking you not to be?"

"You are."

"I am not. I don't want you to go along with the crowd. I want you to be your own man. Stand out in your own way."

"You *do*?"

"Of course I do. Take your plate out to the kitchen."

"Just give me a little longer to find out who I am," I said, heading for the kitchen door while the getting was good.

"Be yourself! Be individualistic!" he called after me. "But for God's sake get your hair cut. You look like an oddball."

"How nice of you to remember to bring your plate out," the Old Lady said, squirting some whipped cream out of a can. "Are you going to have dessert?"

"No, Mom."

She looked me over carefully, checking for any clues as to what mood I left Bore in.

"Your father's a little tired tonight. Maybe you'd better go over to a friend's house to do your homework? I mean he's worked hard, and I don't think we should aggravate him, do you?"

"No, Mom."

"Would you like a glass of wine?" Mr. Pignati offered, straightening up a few things in the living room. It ws great how happy he was to see us. I can't remember Bore, or my mother either for that matter, ever looking happy to see me, let alone when I came into the house with a friend.

"That would be pleasant," Lorraine said.

"This is a great house you've got," I said. "It's well . . . interesting."

He beamed.

"Come on, and I'll show you around," he said, smiling to beat the band.

He took us through the downstairs part, and the less you know about that the better. The first time we were there we saw the hallway when we came in and the stairs that went to the upper floor—and the living room that was really lived in. There was also this dining room affair with the kind of furniture you see everybody put out on the street for the Sanitation Department in the spring.

Then on the other side there was a door leading to a porchlike room that looked like someone had tried to fix it up so it could be lived in but had failed. And the only other thing on the first floor was a kitchen, and that's where we stopped because Lorraine was hungry. I mean, we were really making ourselves at home there after awhile. At first we had just stood around, bashful about touching his things. We'd walk over to a bookcase and touch a book and stroll by a table and admire the handle on a drawer. But in fifteen minutes we were laughing with the Pigman like it was a treasure hunt, and he kept smiling and saying, "Just make yourself at home. You just go right ahead and make yourself at home." But it was really all a lot of junk. The most interesting thing I found was a table drawer full of old *Popular Mechanics* magazine, and the most interesting thing Lorraine found was the icebox.

"Try some of this," Mr. Pignati insisted, holding up a bowl of little roundish things that looked as if they were in a spaghetti sauce.

"*Ummmm!*" Lorraine muttered as she stuffed a few into her mouth. "What are they?"

"Scungilli," the Pigman said. "They're like snails."

"May I use your bathroom?" Lorraine asked her face turning stark white.

"Right upstairs."

Mr. Pignati and I went into the room with all the pigs, and I started lifting the bigger ones to see what country they were made in.

You could hear Lorraine upstairs for about five minutes. When she came downstairs, she had this picture in her hands.

"Who's this?"

There was a pause. Then the smile faded off the Pigman's face. He took the picture from her and moved over to the stuffed armchair and sat down.

"My wife Conchetta," he said, "in her confirmation dress."

"Conchetta?" Lorraine repeated nervously. We both knew something was wrong but couldn't put our finger on it. I got the idea that maybe his wife had run off to California and left him. I mean, you couldn't blame her when you stop to think that her husband's idea of a big time was to go to the zoo and feed a baboon.

"She liked that picture because of the dress," he went on. "It was the only picture she ever liked of herself."

He got up and put it in the table drawer where all those old *Popular Mechanics* books were, and when he turned around, his eyes looked like he was going to start crying. Suddenly he forced a smile and said, "Go upstairs and look around while I get you some wine. Please feel at home, please. . . ."

Then he went down the hall toward the kitchen.

"What else is up there?" I whispered to Lorraine.

"I don't know."

I decided to take a look, but frankly there wasn't much to look at. At the top of the stairs was this plain old bathroom with a shower curtain that had all kinds of fish designs on it.

When I opened the door on the left, I got a little bit scared because there was one of those adjustable desk lamps with a long neck that made it look like a bird about to attack. I put the light on though, and the room was a huge bore. The ceiling slanted on the far side, and there was only one window. It was okay if you wanted to keep somebody as the Prisoner of Zenda, but it looked like a rotten place to work. All it had was this big desk made by taking a thick piece of plywood and laying it over two wooden horses, and a bookcase with blueprints and stuff in it, and a big oscilloscope, with its guts hanging out, in the corner. There were three old TV sets too, but they looked like they didn't even work.

Then I went into the room on the right of the hall. It was a bedroom—much neater than the rest of the house—and it had a lot of drawers and things to go through.

The bedroom had a closet too, so I started with that. There were all kinds of dresses in it, and lacy ladies' coats, and hats that looked like they must have been the purple rage at the turn of the tenth century. It was a big loss; it really was. And let me tell you, this room was a little nerve-racking too. It had a double bed with a cover made of millions of ruffles, and the way the pillows were laid out, it looked like there might be a dead body underneath. I checked that out right away, but there were only pillows. Then I found one drawer in the dresser bureau that had a lot of papers in it.

There were some pictures, and I looked at them quickly. Also there were some bills and old letters and things tied up with a putrid ribbon and then— sort of funny—this little pamphlet caught my eye. It was called *WHAT EVERY FAMILY SHOULD KNOW*. That's all there was on the cover, and it really had my curiosity up, so I opened it. The very first page gave me the creeps.

I ditched that quick enough, but one thought struck me about that dumb high school I go to. They think they're so smart giving the kids garbage like *Johnny Tremain* and *Giants in the Earth* and *Macbeth*, but do you know, I don't think there's a single kid in that whole joint who would know what to do if somebody dropped dead.

In the same drawer there was a leather case with a broken thingamajig to close it, and it had jewelry in it—a lot of junky women's jewelry that looked like it was made out of paste and stuff. I mean, that wife of his—Mr. Pignati's wife—looked like she didn't take anything with her to California. All those clothes in the closet. But how was I supposed to know? Maybe she went to visit the Pigman's sister in a nudist camp or something. They do anything in California— crazy religions and that kind of thing.

Questions

What should be done first?

Who is our Funeral Director?

Do we have a cemetery preference?

Are there any organizations or friends to invite?

What kind and type of casket?

Do we have money for the expense?

If so, where? How much?

If not, where is the money to come from:

Veterans' benefits?

Social Security?

Insurance?

These, and many more, are the questions that are asked when the time comes. Peace of mind will be yours if you follow this booklet.

If you need more than one book, just call the Silver Lake Company, and we will forward it at once.

Silver Lake

(Where Service Comes First)

Funeral Directors
AUTHORIZATION OF SERVICES

NOTE AND TERMS

I/We, the undersigned, individually and jointly hereby authorize The Silver Lake, Co. to direct the funeral of: *Conchetta Pignati* and to provide all professional services, facilities, equipment, and other merchandise and services as set forth above for an agreed consideration of $ 1,321.06 , and in addition thereto a reasonable charge for such other items as may be ordered or any cash advanced by us.

Signed,

Angelo Pignati

190 Howard Avenue

Then I found this bill right in with all the jewelry and junk and her Social Security card, and that's when I knew Conchetta Pignati was not in California. I knew that where Conchetta Pignati was she was never coming back.

8

"His wife's *dead!*" John whispered.

"What?"

"I just found her funeral bill."

A terrible chill ran through me when he said that, because I had been afraid Conchetta was not away on a vacation. I didn't exactly suspect Mr. Pignati of having murdered her and sealed her body behind a wall in the cellar, but I was suspicious. There was something about the glaze in his eyes when he laughed that disturbed me because I could tell he didn't really believe his own laughter. It was a nervous type of laughing, the same kind as that of a landlady we once had after her husband died in a dentist's chair while he was under gas.

"Did you see the ad in yesterday's paper?" Mr. Pignati asked, finally coming back with more of the red wine.

"No."

"For sale: Complete set of encyclopedias, never used. Wife knows everything." And then he let out that laugh again.

I just couldn't smile at his joke. I thought it was very sad. I mean, that cute little girl in the ruffled dress had already grown up, gotten married, lived her life, and was underground somewhere. And Mr. Pignati wasn't able to admit it. That landlady used to think her husband was going to come back one day too, but she died less than two months after him. I've always wondered about those cases where a man and wife die within a short time of each other. Sometimes it's only days. It makes me think that the love between a man and a woman must be the strongest thing in the world.

But then look at my father and mother, although maybe they didn't ever really love each other. Maybe that's why she got the way she is.

"I found this upstairs." John smiled, holding a small plastic card. "What is it?"

The Pigman explained what a charge card was.

"You mean you just sign your name, and a department store lets you take whatever you want, and you don't have to pay for it for months?" John asked, wide-eyed.

Mr. Pignati said he only got the card so his wife could go shopping in the fancy-food delicatessen they've got at Beekman's.

"She loves delicacies," he said.

And I remembered the taste of the scungilli.

When I got home that night, I thought of them again, but another thought struck me. I realized how many things the Pigman and his wife must have shared—even the fun of preparing food. Good food is supposed to produce good conversation, I've heard. I guess it's no wonder my mother and I never had an interesting conversation when all we eat is canned soup, chop suey, and instant coffee. I think I would have learned how to cook if she had ever encouraged me, but the one time I tried baking a cake she said it tasted horrible and was a waste of money.

"Did you fix my coffee?"

"Yes."

"This one has sex on the brain. He has only got a couple of months to live, and he's still got itchy fingers." I watched my mother powdering her nose at the kitchen table. She leaned forward between sips of coffee, dabbing at her face.

"The last nurse quit because she couldn't control his hands. He's always trying to touch something, but I put a stop to that the first time he tried anything."

"Can I make you some eggs?"

"Don't bother. I'll have breakfast at their house. His wife is treating me with kid gloves because they know a nurse isn't easy to come by—particularly when they've got to put up with what I've got to. Make yourself something."

"I'm not hungry."

"Make sure you scrub the kitchen floor today. In fact I'd concentrate on the kitchen. It's worse than anything else."

"We're out of cleanser. Shall I buy a can?"

"Wait until I see if I can take one from the job. I think I saw some when I was going through the closets yesterday." She checked herself in the bathroom mirror and then headed for the door. "Give me a kiss—and lock the doors and windows. Don't open for anyone, do you hear me?"

"Yes, Mother."

"If a salesman rings the bell, don't answer it."

I watched her waiting on the corner until the bus came. If I strained my neck, I could always catch a glimpse of her standing there in her white uniform and white shoes—and she usually wore a short navy-blue jacket, which looked sort of strange over all that white. As I watched her I remembered all the times she said how hard it was to be a nurse—how bad it was for the legs, how painful the varicose veins were that nurses always got from being on their feet so much. I could see her standing under the street light . . . just standing there until the bus came. It was easy to feel sorry for her, to see how awful her life was—even to understand a little why she picked on me so. It hadn't always been like that though.

But she did pick on me now!

Lots of times I'd cry myself to sleep, but more and more I felt myself thinking of the Pigman whenever I felt sad. Sometimes just after I put the light out, I'd see his face smiling or his eyes gleaming as he offered me the snails—some little happy detail I thought I had forgotten—and I'd wish my mother were more like him. I'd wish she knew how to have a little fun for a change.

I got most of the work done in plenty of time for John and me to meet the Pigman down at the Staten Island ferryhouse by eleven thirty that morning. Mr. Pignati said he'd meet us there after he had stopped at the zoo to feed Bobo, which was fine with John. He loves to wait for people in the ferryhouse because all the bums and drunks come over. He really drives them crazy. They've got drunks and bums all over the Staten Island ferryhouse, but not half as many as they've got on the other side at South Ferry. John makes them tell their whole life story before he'll give them a nickel.

This one bum who came over said his name was Dixie. Everybody called him Dixie because he came

from the South. Then he told this story about how
he used to be a professor at Southern Pines University,
but he took some LSD as part of an experimental
program and lost his power of concentration. His
whole academic life had come to an end because
he'd lost his power of concentration.

I thought of writing a story about him until John
told me the same bum had come up to him a month
ago and said his name was Confederate. He said
they called him that because he was from the South.
John said he told an entirely different story—about
how he had been taking a speed-reading course and
he was reading faster than anybody in the world.
He said he used to read so fast he had to buy two
copies of every book and cut the pages out and put
them on tables around the room, and then he'd run
by the pages. That's how fast he could read. He said
he was written up in *Scientific American* magazine
in the January, 1949, issue, and anybody could check
it out. He was supposed to have a sister in Marlboro,
Vermont, who could do the same thing. And then
the tragedy was supposed to have happened. He
was running around the room so fast he banged into
a table and lost his power of concentration.

The Pigman got there in time for us to get the
eleven forty-five boat to Manhattan. I just had to go
along on this trip to Beekman's Department Store
because John has absolutely no control over himself.
If I had let him and Mr. Pignati go alone, John would
have charged half the store. He wouldn't have done
it to be mean. He just isn't used to people giving
him stuff, and that's what Mr. Pignati wanted to do.

When the ferry docked on the other side, we got
off on the upper deck, which meant we had to walk

down this long, curving ramp that looks like a poor man's Guggenheim Museum. The subway station is right there, so we went down the stairs and got on the Seventh Avenue Local. When you take the Seventh Avenue Local, you have to switch at Chambers Street for the Seventh Avenue Express. It really can get boring unless you keep your eyes open. There was one woman at Chambers Street who was talking to herself a mile a minute, and I know now it was another omen.

"Death is coming," she kept repeating. "God told me death is coming. He calls me his little chatty doll . . . God's chatty doll. . . ."

It's sort of spooky how when you're caught talking to God nowadays everybody thinks you're nuts. They used to call you a prophet.

We couldn't get to Thirty-fourth Street quick enough for me, and just as we came up out of the subway, there was Beekman's—good old Beekman's.

Mr. Pignati started getting excited when we got inside with all those Saturday shoppers. You could tell right off he was going to show us around as though he owned the place. He took us right to the fancy-food store on the eighth floor. It was probably the only part of Beekman's he'd ever been to, and I could just picture Conchetta and him pushing the cart up and down the aisles picking out all that vile food.

"Wait until you try these frogs' legs," he said happily, "with ricotta cheese."

I felt sick.

He also picked out three jars of bean soup, bamboo shoots, fish killies with their heads still on, and a lot of other delicious items.

"The killies are tasty in bean soup."

I guess Conchetta and he had liked the same things.

"Now you pick out some things *you'd* like to try." He smiled at me. John had already picked out a carton of tiger's milk and a box of chocolate-covered ants. *Ugh.* Anything to be weird.

"*Please,*" Mr. Pignati insisted.

Just then my eye caught a two-pound can of Love'n Nuts, which is a mixture of pecans, almonds, and popcorn. Right next to it was a large container of Jamboree Juicy Jellies, and before I knew what had happened the Pigman had grabbed them and put them into the shopping cart.

"I don't want you spending all that money, Mr. Pignati," I said.

"Nonsense," he insisted.

But I really didn't. And still it felt good. No one had ever bought me stuff like this before—something I just liked and didn't need and didn't even ask for. Now I knew how John felt because I felt the same way.

After we finished with the delicatessen department, we went to the fifth floor. We had to cut through women's underwear to get to the toy department.

"Hi, doll," John said to one of the dummies that was wearing only a girdle and a brassiere.

"Can I help you, sir?" a saleslady with too much makeup and an enormous beehive hairdo wanted to know.

"I don't think so," I said.

"Nothing for your daughter?" she asked Mr. Pignati. He started to smile.

"I'm not his daughter," I blurted out, and the Pigman looked depressed. I didn't mean to say it as though I would be ashamed to be his daughter, but I guess it just came out that way.

"I'm his niece," I quickly offered, returning the smile to Mr. Pignati's face.

"Is there something you'd like here?" Mr. Pignati asked, and I knew he meant it. I had no intention of accepting anything more, but I couldn't help looking around.

"No, nothing, thank you."

"We have some lovely nylon stockings," the saleslady said, with just the tone to make me embarrassed if I didn't say yes.

"Go ahead," Mr. Pignati urged. "Please."

"I'll take one pair," I mumbled, and I'm sure my face was stark red.

"They come in three-pair packages."

"We'll take three pairs," the Pigman insisted.

"What size, please?"

"Eleven."

"*Eleven?*"

"Yes, ma'am. Eleven," I repeated.

"You couldn't take more than a size seven-and-a-half."

"I want size eleven, thank you."

"But—"

"Size *eleven.*"

I began to get terrified at what my mother would say when I brought her home three pairs of stockings. I'd have to tell her some girl friend at school bought them by mistake and wanted to sell them cheap or something like that. But then I broke out laughing.

"Is something funny?" the saleslady inquired, putting her hand up to her beehive.

"No," I said, watching John slip a lit cigarette into the hand of the dummy with the girdle and the brassiere.

The visit to the toy department was something else. I hadn't been in Beekman's toy department in years, not since I was three years old and my mother took me to sit on Santa Claus' lap. It was fun then, but now everything was made out of cheap plastic, and you could tell the stuff would break in a minute.

The one thing that really got my goat was these ships in bottles. They were ships in bottles all right, but the bottles were made out of plastic. They had bottoms so you could open the bottle up and take the ship out whenever you felt like it. I mean, they lost the whole point of having a ship in a bottle. You're supposed to wonder about how it got in there, not be able to screw the bottom off the thing and take the ship out whenever you feel like it.

And there was the arsenal of course: guns, pistols, shotguns, slingshots, knives, and swords. It's no wonder kids grow up to be killers with all that rehearsal. There was enough artillery in Beekman's toy department to wipe out Red China and the Mau-Mau tribe of Africa, and I personally think some of the toy manufacturers could use a good course in preventive psychiatry.

"Can we look at the pet shop?" Mr. Pignati asked.

John groaned.

"Of course we can," I said scowling at John.

"*Kitchykitchykitchykoo,*" John said, tapping his finger on the side of an aquarium that had two piranha flesh-eating fish in it. One of them darted for his finger and bumped its nose on the glass.

Next to them were three little monkeys in a cage that were hugging each other like crazy, and you-know-who stopped to talk to them for half an hour.

"Bobo . . . you look just like my little Bobo," Mr. Pignati was saying, leaning over the counter and waving his hand at one of the poor monkeys that looked like it was on the verge of a nervous breakdown.

"My little Bobo."

The three monkeys were hugging each other desperately, and I really had to smile, watching them. Here they were, clinging to each other in the pet shop at Beekman's, looking out at everybody with these tiny, wet eyes—as though pleading for love. They looked so lonely and sweet just holding on to each other.

"Aren't they cute?" I had to say.

"Bobo . . . you look like my little Bobo—"

"Give 'em a piece of popcorn," John suggested. I offered my can of Love'n Nuts to Mr. Pignati, and he took a couple of pieces.

"Don't feed them," this nasty floorwalker called out.

"I'm sorry," Mr. Pignati said, looking embarrassed.

"Why not?" John had to ask.

"Because I told you not to, that's why."

Now that's the kind of logic that really sets John off. That floorwalker could have simply said that monkeys bite or that popcorn is not their natural diet or something like that—but instead he had to think he was a schoolteacher. From that moment on, every time the floorwalker half turned his back John made believe he was throwing popcorn into the monkey cage, and I thought that man was going to go insane.

"Bobo. Little Bobo. . . ."

I made the mistake of leaving the two of them alone while I went to the ladies' room, because when I came out John was yelling, "Hurry up!"

"What for?"

"Mr. Pignati's going to buy us roller skates."

"Oh, no, he isn't. He's spent enough money on us."

"He's not spending any money," John corrected. "He's going to charge them!" He ran ahead and caught up with the Pigman, who was heading for the sports department.

"How do those fit?" the salesman asked.

"Mr. Pignati, I don't think you should buy these."

"I used to love roller-skating," he answered. He looked so happy and funny bending over in his seat, trying to put on one of the skates, that I had to laugh. One part of me was saying "Don't let this nice old man waste his money," and the other half was saying "Enjoy it, enjoy doing something absolutely absurd"—something that let me be a child in a way I never could be with my mother, something just silly and absurd and . . . beautiful.

"Please let me get them," Mr. Pignati said, practically asking for my permission.

"I'll wear mine," John told the salesman, a tiny round bald man with spectacles which quickly dropped to the end of his nose as he laced up the skates.

"Pardon me?"

John picked up his shoes and plopped them into the box the shoe skates came in. "I said I'm going to wear them."

"But you're on the fifth floor."

"She'll wear hers too."

"John, are you crazy?" Just as the words came out of my mouth I could tell from the fallen expression on his face that if I didn't wear the roller skates, I'd be letting him down. I'd be disappointing him in the main thing that he liked about me. I—and maybe now even the Pigman—were the only ones he knew who could understand that doing something like roller-skating out of Beekman's was not absolutely crazy. Everything in his home had to have a purpose. There was no one there who could understand doing something just for fun—something crazy —and that was what he'd liked about me from that first day when I laughed on the bus and was just as crazy as he was.

"I'll wear mine too," I sighed, and before long we were rolling toward the escalator—a good number of people staring.

"Wait for me," Mr. Pignati yelled, carrying his skates under his arm and laughing along with us.

All John was doing was opening his arms and in his own way saying: "Look at me, world! Look at my life and energy and how glad I am to be alive!" We must have looked just like three monkeys. The Pigman, John, and me—three funny little monkeys.

DEAR ALICE
by Alice Vandenberg

HE LOVES DOLLS

DEAR ALICE: My husband and I have just had another violent fight concerning our five-year-old son Timothy, and I desperately need your advice.

My son adores playing with a doll I bought for him last Xmas. He spends hours with it, putting doll clothes on it, and feeding it on doll dishes. This aggravates his father no end, and several other adults have made nasty remarks about it, too.

Personally, I see nothing wrong with Timothy playing with this doll because it is a sailor doll. He puts a cute little white hat and uniform on it and I think the image is totally masculine. Why, if a woman plays Cowboy and Indians, everyone says she's a darling little tomboy, but when a boy plays with a doll they say he's queer? Please answer this.

WORRIED MOTHER

9

I cut that "Dear Alice" thing out because it reminded me of Norton, and there are a few other things I've got to tell you about him because he gets involved in this memorial epic a little later on.

Lorraine told you she thinks Norton and I hate each other. It's true. Norton is so low on the scale of evolution he belongs back in the age of the Cro-Magnon man.

Norton actually did play with dolls when he was a kid. That was his mother's fault, just like in that "Dear Alice" column. When he was old enough to know better, he didn't play with dolls anymore. But the kids used to make cracks about him, so that made him go beserk around the age of ten. He was the only berserk ten-year-old in the neighborhood. From then on he turned tough guy all the way. He was always picking fights and throwing stones and beating up everybody. In fact, he got so tough he used to go around calling the other guys sissies.

When I was a freshman going through my Bathroom-Bomber complex, Norton was a specialist in the five-finger discount. He used to shoplift everywhere he went. It used to be small-time stuff like costume jewelry for his mother and candy bars and newspapers. Then he got even worse, until now his eyes even drift out of focus when you're talking to him. He's the type of guy who could grow up to be a killer.

Now you can understand why I was suspicious when Norton invited me to the cemetery to have a beer just before Thanksgiving. That was more than a month after Lorraine and I first met the Pigman.

"How come you're going over there all the time?" Norton finally blurted out as he opened up a bottle of a putrid brand of beer and made believe he was deeply interested in looking down into one of the glass domes on top of Masterson's tomb.

"Where?"

He looked me straight in the eye for a second, and then one of his eyes moved away. "You know where— that old guy's house on Howard Avenue."

"Oh him."

"Is he queer or something?"

"He's just a nice guy."

"What's his house like?"

"Like?"

"Has he got anything worth stealing?" Norton clarified, his eyes beginning to get mean and sneaky like an alley cat about to jump on a bird.

"Naw," I muttered, throwing a pebble down off the front of the tomb. "All he's got are some tools and stuff—"

"Tools? Norton perked up. "What kind of tools?"

"Just some electrical junk."

"DD's been asking for a lot of that electric stuff. There's a big market for electronics, you know."

As soon as he mentioned DD I felt like socking him right in the face. I mean, DD is this lunatic man on Richmond Avenue who makes believe he's the leader of organized crime on Staten Island, but all he handles are the hubcaps and radios that kids steal. King of the kids.

"Any TV's or radios?"

"No," I said.

Norton had reached a new peak of ugliness that day with the afternoon sun shining down on him. He paused a minute, then took a sip of his beer.

"Well, what are you and that screech owl going over there for?"

"I told you not to call Lorraine a screech owl!"

"What if I feel like calling her a screech owl?"

I took a sip of my beer, which was as warm as @#$%, and then looked him straight in the face. I wasn't scared of him because we were sort of evenly matched.

"I mean, what would you *do* about it?" Norton grinned.

"Oh, probably nothing," I said, smiling back at him. "Maybe I'd go buy some ... marshmallows."

The grin on Norton's face faded away so quickly you'd think I just stuck a knife into him. "You wouldn't happen to know where I could buy some ... marshmallows, would you?" I said, smiling.

"All right, I'm sorry I called her a screech owl," Norton said, trying to avoid the unavoidable.

"You got anything more to say to me?" I said, standing up.

"Yeah." Norton nodded slowly and with a return of courage said, "if you don't give me a little more information about that old goat, maybe Dennis and me will pay a little visit over there ourselves."

I yawned and stretched my arms into the air. "Well, I can see this conference is over. Thanks for the beer." Then I threw my empty bottle way in

back of the tomb. I mean, I was really furious by
this time, and I started walking down the path from
the top and out across the white gravel courtyard.

"Maybe we'll pay a visit real soon!" Norton called
out, and I turned to see him standing on top of
the tomb. I walked a few steps farther so that I
was about a hundred yards or so away, and then I
spun around.

"You do that," I yelled at the top of my lungs.
"You do that, you Marshmallow Kid!"

I knew Norton had to make believe he didn't
hear that last remark because he would have had to
run after me and try to bash my head in with a rock
otherwise. It's like paranoia in reverse when people
are really calling you insulting things and you
deliberately pretend they aren't.

But I guess I'm just as screwed up as he is.

Sometimes I try to figure out why I'm the way I
am. Take my drinking for instance.

"Johnny wants a sip of beer," Bore used to say in
the old days. He got a big kick out of it when I was
about ten years old, and I'd go around emptying all
the beer glasses lying around the house.

"That kid's going to be a real drinker," he'd say
in front of company, and then I'd go through my
beer-drinking performance for everybody, and they'd
laugh their heads off. It was about the only thing
I ever did that got any attention. My brother was
the one everybody really liked—Kenny, the smart
college kid. The only thing I did better than him
was drink beer.

"A chip off the old block."

Some chip.

When Bore got sclerosis of the liver like Lorraine
told you, he stopped drinking, but I didn't. I don't

think I know exactly what year I noticed it, but then all of a sudden Bore and the Old Lady got old. They didn't fight anymore. They didn't do much of anything anymore, which is why I guess I nicknamed them the way I did. They just seemed tired, and I seemed out of place in the house. I had become a disturbing influence, as they say. If I light up a cigarette, all my mother's really worried about is that I'm going to burn a hole in the rug. If I want a beer, she's worried I'm not going to rinse the glass out.

"John, turn your radio down."

"John, you're disturbing your father."

"John, you're disturbing your mother."

"John, you're disturbing the cat."

"John, don't slam the door when you go out; don't make so much noise on the porch; don't bang your feet when you walk up the stairs; don't walk on the kitchen floor—don't, don't, don't."

"John, please do whatever you like. Make yourself comfortable. If you want something out of the refrigerator, help yourself. I want you to feel at home."

And always with a big smile so you knew he meant it

That was the Pigman, and I knew I'd kill Norton if he tried to hurt the old man.

10

It got so that every day John and I would go over to the Pigman's after school and have a glass of wine and conversation. It was routine by the time the Christmas holidays came around, and it was nice to have some place to go besides the cemetery when it was cold out. Masterson's tomb is an escapist's dream in the summer, but it's a realist's nightmare in December.

"Where have you been?"

"I told you the Latin Club was meeting today— and then I missed the bus coming home."

I went right into the bedroom and took off my coat.

"Did I see you in a car today?" my mother asked, coming to the doorway to watch my reaction. "I was waiting for you to go to the store. When you didn't come home, I walked down myself, and I saw a girl in a car that looked just like you." She was holding the large coffee cup and stirring nervously.

"It wasn't me."

"I didn't think it was. You know very well what I'd do if I ever caught you in a car."

"Yes, Mother."

"Be a good girl and iron my uniform, will you?

I came home late last night," she went on, following me into the kitchen, "and the girl down the street was in a car, necking like a slut."

"Maybe she's engaged to that boy."

"I don't care. Just don't let me catch you in a car if you know what's good for you. I got some shrimp chop suey from the Chinese restaurant. I saved yours, but get the uniform done first."

She always warns me about getting into cars and things like that. When she goes to work on a night shift, she constantly reminds me to lock the doors and windows, and sometimes she calls on the phone if she gets a chance and tells me again. Beware of men is what she's really saying. They have dirty minds, and they're only after one thing. Rapists are roaming the earth.

But now I understand her a little. I think the only man she really hates is my father—even though he's dead. I don't think she'll ever be able to forgive what he did to her. She used to put me through the story at least twice a year—how when she was pregnant with me her doctor called and told her my father had some kind of disease, and she shouldn't let him touch her until he got rid of it. It turned out that he had a girl friend on the side, and that's when she filed for a legal separation. Everyone was surprised, because they had been childhood sweethearts, as the expression goes. It must have been awful for her when she found out about him. She never talks about him now—just how awful men are in general. She's what the psychologists call fixated on the subject.

There's one picture of my mother and father in an album, which is how I like to remember them. He's wearing a football uniform—a handsome young man—with his arm around her. She's wearing one of those funny racoon coats. They're smiling at each other in a grass field somewhere in Stapleton.

"I got a run in one of the new stockings last night. I didn't notice it until I washed them this morning." I could tell from the way she spoke that it was her way of thanking me for giving them to her. "Where did you get the money for them?"

"I told you."

"Tell me again."

"I walked to school a few days instead of taking the bus."

"You said you skipped lunch."

"*And* I skipped lunch a couple of times."

She mulled that over a few seconds, but she had to get to work on time and couldn't devote her full energies to interrogating. She always makes me tell the same story over a week or so later to see if I slip up on any details.

"When I give you money for the bus, you ride the bus. It doesn't look right for a girl to be walking along the streets."

"Yes, Mother."

"It looks like you're trying to get picked up."

So, all things considered, it was wonderful getting over to Mr. Pignati's for a little dash of wine every day.

"Please don't bring anything," the Pigman always pleaded. "Just let me know what you want, and I'll get it for you."

I was surprised to see John break down and start buying his own six-packs of beer. I really was. I had been bringing things like potato chips and pretzels all along simply because I felt funny mooching off Mr. Pignati.

"We want to bring our own stuff from now on."

"Whenever we can," John added quickly.

So things were really going along fine until one Sunday night in January when there was a snow-storm—and the Pigman had been to the zoo. John and I got over to the house around eight o'clock and were all set to watch a television show when we noticed Mr. Pignati was sad as all get out. I don't even want to tell you this part, but one of us has to. It's very depressing; it really is.

The minute we walked into the house I knew there was something wrong with him. He looked sick. Just worn out and sick, even though he was trying to smile, and you could tell he was feeling low. I told him to stay in his chair and I'd get the refreshments, and he looked rather grateful for my offer.

"Bobo wouldn't eat today," he said, forcing a weak smile. "I offered him a chocolate bar, and he just let it drop outside the cage."

I went out to the kitchen and left John and the Pigman watching some kind of TV spectacular, the theme of which was *Hurrah for Hollywood*. Everybody was in it, so I knew it was going to be a strenuous bore.

"Bobo's getting old. . . ." I heard Mr. Pignati say as I served him a glass of wine. John had a can of beer, and I just didn't feel like anything at that moment.

"Who?" John asked, not moving his eyes from the TV screen.

"Bobo. . . ."

I sat in a creaky wooden chair near the window, and I could feel a terrible draft. Outside, the snow was falling, and it looked very pretty. There were a lot of pine trees, and the snow was sticking to them.

It dawned on me then what a strain it must have been on Mr. Pignati to have trudged all the way down to see the baboon. He had even shoveled the walk outside, which I knew was for us. And just at that moment, for no reason at all, I remembered the old lady at Chambers Street saying "Death is coming."

"Anybody hungry?" I asked, going out to the kitchen again without waiting for an answer. I came back with some candy on a plate. All I wanted was to cheer everybody up. The TV was certainly doing the best it could, with a blond starlet singing "Hurrah for Hollywood . . . La-La-La-De-Dum" as two hundred chorus boys lifted her up into the air.

"Have a piece of candy?" I asked, offering the plate to John. He was so hypnotized by that starlet he simply reached over and grabbed a piece and stuck it in his mouth without looking. Then a comedian finally told a joke we laughed at.

"John," I whispered, "I think right now is a good time." I got up and turned the TV down and waited for John to start. He looked very nervous over what we had decided to tell the Pigman.

"Mr. Pignati—"

"Yes?"

"Mr. Pignati, there's something Lorraine and I think we should tell you."

Mr. Pignati looked very serious and worried.

"Just tell him, John."

"Well, Mr. Pignati," he started, taking a big puff on his cigarette, "Lorraine and I have something on our consciences that you ought to know about."

"Will you just tell him?"

He took another puff on his cigarette.

"You've been so nice to us that we want to be honest with you—"

"Yes?" Mr. Pignati said, sitting forward in his chair.

"You see, Mr. Pignati, we're not charity workers."

He just stared at us.

"We're high-school kids," John added a little nervously. "We're sorry we lied to you."

The Pigman looked so sad, and it didn't seem like it was just because of our confession. It looked like there was so much more going on in his mind.

I couldn't keep from speaking. "It was a game," I offered, and I felt myself talking on and on, trying to put things on a lighter level. "We didn't do it to be mean," I said at last.

"No," John spoke up. "Honest."

"We just had to be honest with you because we like you more than anyone we know."

Finally we had to stop talking and wait for some response from him. He had turned his head away and seemed to be looking out the window. Perhaps John had been right when he said we should've forgotten the whole thing—never mentioned it. Maybe there are some lies you should never admit to. I had told him we had to be truthful, and now I was sorry because I think I knew before the Pigman opened his mouth what he would have to tell us in return.

"She used to keep the house so clean," Mr. Pignati muttered, lowering his head.

I squirmed slightly.

"Who?"

"Conchetta. . . ."

John looked at me and I looked at him. It was the first time the Pigman had mentioned her in months.

"I had them make a cake—"

"Pardon me, Mr. Pignati," I said softly, "a cake?"

"I had them make a cake . . . the bakery . . . for our anniversary." He wiped his eyes with a wrinkled handkerchief he took from one of his pockets. "Something like our wedding cake was, with a girl in white on top . . . and a boy."

I held my breath.

"She loved me . . ." he said. He looked so tired.

"We loved each other. We didn't need anyone else. She did everything for me. We were each other's life," he managed to say and then broke into sobs. He tried to cover his eyes and turn his head so we wouldn't have to see him like that.

I couldn't help thinking about my mother and father—that maybe as simple as Mr. Pignati was, he knew something about love and having fun that other people didn't. I guess Conchetta had known the secret too.

Mr. Pignati raised his head slowly and looked at us, tears pouring down his face. John pretended not to notice by watching the television, but I knew he really wasn't. He might have been thinking about his parents too.

I went over and put my hand on Mr. Pignati's. There was nothing else I could think of doing. *Tell us*, I wanted to say to him, tell us if it'll make you feel better.

"She's dead," he said, wiping his tears with the large white handkerchief.

There was a pause, and then John turned to the Pigman. "We're sorry," he said, in such a gentle way I wanted to kiss him for it. There was no need to say anything more.

Hurrah for Hollywood was still blasting away, but now there were two thousand chorus boys swinging the blond into the air. I tried to think of something to say.

"Have another piece of candy, John?"

Without looking at the Pigman or me, he reached over and took it.

"What kind of candy is this?"

"Chocolate-covered ants."

You never saw anybody run faster for the kitchen sink in your life, and at last there was a laugh out of Mr. Pignati. I was so relieved he had laughed that I'd have eaten snails and scungilli or anything else. Ants were nothing. Even the Pigman and I tried one of the chocolates, which tasted a little like candy with crispy rice.

"You louse!" I heard a call from the kitchen as I stuffed another little square of ants into my mouth. They really were rather tasty.

John took extra long coming back, and I could hear him getting his roller skates out of the closet in the back room where all the pigs were. I knew he'd have to do something to try to top my little ant joke. So when he came flying into the living room on skates, I laughed it up so he'd feel a little better about my slipping him the insects. Then the Pigman wanted to get in on the act. That's how the three of us were. If one of us did something that was funny, the other two had to come up with something too. Three copycats. It wasn't exactly that we had to show off so much as that we wanted to entertain each other. We wanted to show equally how much we were thankful for each other's company.

Well, the Pigman passed out pencils and paper, so I knew it was going to be one of those games like how to memorize ten items.

"Number from one to five." The Pigman started getting a little bit of the old gleam back. "This is going to tell you what kind of a person you are." He drew a diagram on a piece of paper and laid it in front of us. I thought he had completely flipped.

"I'm going to tell you a murder story, and your job is just to listen." When he drew the skull and wrote "ASSASSIN," John perked up a little.

"There is a river with a bridge over it, and a WIFE and her HUSBAND live in a house on one side. The WIFE has a LOVER who lives on the other side of the river, and the only way to get from one side of the river to the other is to walk across the bridge or to ask the BOATMAN to take you.

"One day the HUSBAND tells his WIFE that he has to be gone all night to handle some business in a faraway town. The WIFE pleads with him to take her with him because she knows if he doesn't she will be unfaithful to him. The HUSBAND absolutely refuses to take her because she will only be in the way of his important business.

"So the HUSBAND goes alone. When he is gone, the WIFE goes over the bridge and stays with her LOVER. The night passes, and dawn is almost up when the WIFE leaves because she must get back to her own house before her HUSBAND gets home. She starts to cross the bridge but sees an ASSASSIN waiting for her on the other side, and she knows if she tries to cross, he will murder her. In terror, she runs up the side of the river and asks the BOATMAN to take her across the river, but he wants fifty cents. She has no money, so he refuses to take her.

"The wife runs back to the LOVER's house and explains to him what her predicament is and asks

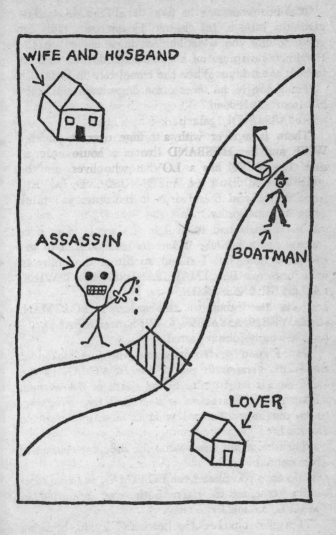

WIFE AND HUSBAND

ASSASSIN

BOATMAN

LOVER

him for fifty cents to pay the BOATMAN. The LOVER refuses, telling her it's her own fault for getting into the situation. As dawn comes up the WIFE is nearly out of her mind and decides to dash across the bridge. When she comes face to face with the ASSASSIN, he takes out a large knife and stabs her until she is dead."

"So what?" John asked.

"Now I want you to write down on the paper I gave you the names of the characters in the order in which you think they were most responsible for the WIFE's death. Just list WIFE, HUSBAND, LOVER, ASSASSIN, and BOATMAN in the order you think they are most guilty."

Mr. Pignati had to explain the whole story over to me again because it was too complicated to get the first time, but I ended up listing the guilty in this order: 1. BOATMAN, 2. HUSBAND, 3. WIFE, 4. LOVER, 5. ASSASSIN.

John listed them in this order: 1. BOATMAN, 2. LOVER, 3. ASSASSIN, 4. WIFE, 5. HUSBAND.

"So what?" John repeated.

Mr. Pignati started laughing when he looked at our lists. "You both picked the BOATMAN as the one who is most guilty in the death of the woman. Each of the characters is a symbol for something, and you have betrayed what is most important to you in life."

Then he wrote down what the different characters represented.

"Because you picked the BOATMAN as being most guilty, that means you're both most interested in MAGIC," he said.

"I'm glad I picked the boatman," I said, blushing a little. The order in which John liked things in the

wife = fun

husband = love

lover = sex

assassin = money

boatman = magic

world was supposed to be magic, sex, money, fun, and love. The order in which I was supposed to prefer these qualities was magic, love, fun, sex, and money. I thought that was sort of accurate, if you ask me.

So John and I laughed a lot for the Pigman, making him think we thought the game was two tons of fun. It wasn't bad, but it certainly wasn't two tons of fun. But he always had to do something to try to top us. The longer he knew us, the more of a kid he became. It was cute in a way.

After Mr. Pignati finished playing the psychological game with us, John started skating. First he skated just in that hall leading from the dining room to the doorway with the curtains where all the pigs were. But then after a few minutes, he started skating right through the living room while Mr. Pignati and I watched television. Finally he opened the door to the porch so that now he had about fifty feet of nice wooden floor to race on. That looked so attractive I went and put my skates on. Mr. Pignati laughed like anything as we went flying by, and before we knew it he had his skates on and the three of us were zooming right from the porch through the living room and dining room down the hall into the room with the pigs. It was really a scream, particularly when we started playing tag. We were having so much fun I just never thought anyone would hurt himself. I mean, I had forgotten about Mr. Pignati going way down to the zoo in all that snow. I forgot he had shoveled the walk, and I guess for a few minutes I forgot he was so old.

John got particularly wild at one point when Mr. Pignati was *It* and there weren't many obstacles you could skate around on the ground floor except the kitchen table, and that got mundane after awhile. So John was off, running up the stairs to the bedroom with his skates on, and we were all howling with laughter. *Clomp! Clomp!* What a racket those skates made. And Mr. Pignati started right up after him, puffing like crazy, his face redder than a beet. *Clomp! Clomp! Clomp!* right up the stairs.

Suddenly, just a few steps up, Mr. Pignati stopped. He started to gasp for air and turned around to face me at the bottom of the stairs . . . trying to speak. Only a horrible moan came out.

"Bet you can't get me!" John giggled, still clomping up the stairs, not realizing what was going on behind him.

"Mr. Pignati—" I started, the words catching in my throat.

"Bet you can't catch me!"

The Pigman reached his left hand out to me.

"What's the matter?" I yelled.

He started to double over—his eyes fastened on me—gaping like a fish out of water. Then he pressed his right hand to his chest and fell to the bottom of the stairs.

11

I knew it was a heart attack right away. Lorraine almost passed out, but I knew enough to call the police. They got there about ten minutes later with an ambulance from St. Ambrose Hospital, and we almost didn't have enough time to get the skates off.

Two attendants came in with an old lady doctor, and we told them how he had been shoveling snow and had been out all day, and they just whisked him away on a stretcher like an old sack of potatoes. He was breathing just fine. Maybe a little fast, but it certainly didn't look like he was going to die or anything like that.

"Who are you?" this one snotty cop asked.

"His children," I said, and I thought Lorraine was going to collapse with fear. We both knew what her mother would do if she found out.

I answered all the questions he asked, and when I didn't know the answers, I made them up.

"Your father's age?"

"Fifty-eight," I said.

"Wife?"

"Deceased."

"Place of birth?"

"Sorrento."

"You two kids don't look Italian."

"Our mother was Yugoslavian."

I mean those particular cops were so dumb it was pathetic. I felt like I was talking to two grown-up Dennises who had arrested mental growth. It was a big deal over nothing. They wanted to know if we could take care of ourselves, and we assured them we were very mature.

"Your name?"

"John Pignati."

"You?" The cop pointed at Lorraine.

"Lorraine . . . Pignati."

They finally left after they had a good look around the place. I mean, the furnishings were enough to make anybody think a pack of wild gypsies lived there, but they were probably anxious to get along on the rounds of the local bars and collect their graft for the week. Lorraine got furious when I told her that and said she hoped I needed help some day and there were no policemen to call. Then she called me stupid and left me standing in the hall. I walked to the edge of the living room and just waited for the lecture I knew was coming.

"You shouldn't have gone upstairs with the roller skates on," she finally said as though in a trance.

"I didn't think he would follow me up."

"You just never know when to stop."

"Oh, shut up!" I snapped at her. "You're beginning to sound like my Old Lady."

She turned her head away, and I was sorry I had yelled at her. "He's not going to die. It was just a little stroke, that's all. He was breathing fine when they carried him out."

I needed two beers after that, but Lorraine was

nervous about staying there. So we found the keys to the house in the kitchen, locked up, and took a walk in the cemetery. We didn't last long there because it was too cold, and she felt terrible when we walked by a freshly dug grave. There's nothing worse than a freshly dug grave with snow falling on it.

The next day we cut school and took the Number 107 bus to St. Ambrose Hospital. We got there a half hour before visiting time, but that gave us time to check on Mr. Pignati and find out that he wasn't dead. In fact he was so alive he looked better than ever, but I've heard that's the way a lot of people are when they have heart attacks. I mean, that's supposed to be the real danger period because they feel energetic, but if they exert themselves, they can have another attack and croak. This Transylvanian-looking nun-nurse made us sign our names in a book and gave us a couple of passes so everyone at the hospital would know we had permission to be there and were not a couple of ghouls raiding the morgue. I hate to go to hospitals because you never know when you get in one of the elevators if the guy next to you has the galloping bubonic plague.

You should have seen Lorraine carrying eleven gladiolas. She looked like a Mongolian peasant hawking flowers in a flea market. We took them from three different graves in the cemetery and couldn't find a twelfth gladiola anywhere. But who counts a dozen gladiolas when you get them? We still pretended we were John and Lorraine Pignati because only members of the immediate family were allowed to visit.

"Your son and daughter are here," this fat, huge

nurse said, opening the door to Room 304. And there was the Pigman, propped up on his high pillow with the bed raised. It was a semiprivate room, and I'd better not tell you about the other patient in there that made it semiprivate because he looked like he wasn't long for this world. They had a guy with some kind of oxygen-tent thing nearby that looked like a malaria net.

"Hi!" Mr. Pignati said, with a great big grin on his face. You'd have thought he was a guest in a hotel the way he looked, with this breakfast tray right in front of him on a weird-looking bed table.

"Look at the lovely flowers they brought," the fat, huge nurse said. "I'll put them in some water." She flashed a gigantic smile herself and then beat it.

"We had to make believe we were your kids," I explained, and you should have seen him smile.

"Are you all right?" Lorraine asked.

"Of course I'm all right." He laughed. "I'm getting out of here in a few days. There's nothing wrong with me. The doctor even said so."

There was a lot of small talk after that, and Lorraine never took her eyes off the guy in the other bed, who looked like he was 193 years old. Then the fat, huge nurse came back in with the gladiolas in this crummy glass vase that looked like they had just dug it up in the backyard. "Aren't they pretty?" she said and then beat it again.

"Is the house all right?" Mr. Pignati asked.

"We locked it up last night after the cops left," I said.

Lorraine fumbled in her pocketbook. "We brought you the keys," she said, holding them out to him.

"You keep them," he said. "Maybe you'll want to

watch some television or have some more chocolate ants." He laughed as usual.

"I don't think so—"

"Maybe we will," I said, taking the keys right out of her hand. "We can leave them in the mailbox, in case we don't cut school tomorrow."

"I don't think we—"

I flashed Lorraine a dirty look, and she never finished her sentence.

"You're looking good," I commented.

"I'm sorry if I was any trouble yesterday."

"Are you kidding? Lorraine and I thrive on excitement." And then the three of us giggled.

"What did you have for breakfast?" Lorraine inquired, which was a little uncalled-for since all you had to do was look at the tray, and you could tell it was the usual rubbery eggs you always get in a hospital.

"You didn't eat your toast," she further observed.

"Do you think you could stop by and see Bobo for me?"

"Sure," I said.

"Tell him I miss him."

Just then the guy in the other bed took a choking fit, and the three of us just looked very uncomfortable until that was over. The fat nurse came running in and did something to him to make him stop. It looked like she strangled him actually.

"Get him the peanuts in the yellow package— not the red package. He likes the dry-roasted ones better."

"Sure."

"And half a hot dog. Don't give him the whole hot dog because he never eats all of it."

"How are you all doing?" the nurse said, bounding in and exhibiting her ivories again. "Your father's a very funny man," she squealed. "He knows an awful lot of jokes."

"We know."

Then she started cranking the bed.

"A very funny man. . . ."

It was scary the way Mr. Pignati's head seemed to stick out of that mountain of white sheets and just sink slowly downward.

"I think you'd better be going now."

"We're going to miss you, Mr. Pignati," Lorraine said, as though she was giving last rites.

"Please take care of Bobo until I get out." He smiled. "And the house. Make yourselves comfortable and use anything that's there."

"Good-bye, Mr. Pignati."

By the time we left, I was so glad to see the outside world I thought I had been in prison for seventy-three years. The smell of hospitals always makes me think of death. In fact I think hospitals are exactly what graveyards are supposed to be like. They ought to bury people in hospitals and let sick people get well in the cemeteries.

The sun was shining, and the ice was beginning to melt on the street. A big plow came down Forest Avenue, scooping snow right into the front of it and throwing it out the top through this pipe contraption. It looked like a black dragon devouring everything it touched. Pretty soon our bus came along, and then we hiked back up to the house.

Everything that happened from then on Lorraine blames me for, and maybe she's right. Things were just fine at first. Lorraine was in her glory because she had a brainstorm about making spaghetti. That would have been a superb idea if I had overlooked the fact that I loathe spaghetti. Mr. Pignati had some sauce left in the refrigerator, and there were three packages of number nine vermicelli, so I decided to let the little homemaker go ahead with it.

"I miss him," Lorraine sighed, sprinkling salt into the boiling water.

"Who?"

"You know very well *who*."

It was sort of strange without him around. I stayed in the living room and watched television, and when my mentality couldn't stand that any longer, I went upstairs.

"John, what are you doing up there?"

"None of your business."

I went into the bedroom and opened the closet with all of Mr. Pignati's clothes. He didn't have that much, but I knew even if he were next to me, he wouldn't mind if I tried on a jacket or two. My own father won't let me touch his stuff.

I tried on a shiny blue suit that looked so worn I think Columbus must have sported it over to the New World. The lapels were so big I felt as though I was wearing reverse water wings. There was a full-length mirror on the door, and when I saw myself, I realized I wasn't plain old John Conlan anymore. I was a famous actor getting ready to go before the cameras to play the role of a distinguished European businessman and lover.

"The spaghetti's almost ready!"

I took one of his ties that looked like a red-and-blue flowered kite and hung it around my neck, and when I found a makeup pencil on the top of the bureau drawer, my transformation was complete—a moustache.

"Good Lord," Lorraine gulped. I thought she was going to drop the pot of spaghetti. She had set the dining-room table and pulled down the shades so it was pretty shadowy, and that made me look perfect. In the middle of the table were two religious-looking candles burning away.

"You look fantastic!" she blurted.

"You think so?"

"Watch the sauce on the stove. I want to wash my hands upstairs," she said, and I caught a bit of a wicked smile on her face.

The sauce had come to a boil four times, and I had to keep shutting off the heat because the goo was spilling over the edge of the pan.

"Will you hurry up?"

"I'm coming." Lorraine's voice came from the bedroom—as if I didn't know what she was doing.

I finally shut the stove off and went into the living room. I was planning to put the TV on, and I was mad as @#$% because I knew the spaghetti was congealing in the pot. I don't like spaghetti when it's normal, let alone congealed.

"Good evening," came this sexy voice from the stairs.

She stood there for a moment, and I couldn't believe my eyes. I knew she had been digging out some old rags of Conchetta's, but I hadn't expected this. She was wearing a white dress with two million ruffles and a neckline that was the lowest she'd ever worn . . . and makeup and high heels and an ostrich feather in her hair. She looked just like one of those unknown actresses you see on the TV summer-replacement programs.

"You look beautiful!"

"Do you mean it?"

I let out a growl and started toward her, imitating Bobo. She squealed with laughter and ran back up the stairs with me right after her.

"Stop it, John!"

"I am a handsome European businessman, and you are in love with me!"

She tried to hold the bedroom door shut, but I forced it, and she ran to the far side so there was only the bed between us.

"Come to me, my darling!"

We were both laughing so hard we could hardly speak.

"One kiss is all I ask!"

I caught her and threw her on the bed. I could hear the sound of the cameras clicking away on the set.

"One kiss!"

"John, stop it now. I'm not kidding." She started laughing again right in my arms, but I stopped it by putting my lips on hers. It was the first time we had ever kissed. When I moved my lips away from hers, we just looked at each other, and somehow we were not acting anymore.

"I think we'd better go downstairs," Lorraine said.

"All right."

"Dinner is served," she announced, carrying this big plate of congealed spaghetti. We each sat at opposite ends of the table with the candles burning away. I poured us some wine in these long-stemmed glasses, and for a few moments we just sat looking at each other—her with the feather in her hair and me with my moustache.

"To the Pigman," I said softly.

"To the Pigman."

She lifted her glass, and she was lovely.

12

"I wish this one would hurry up and croak because her husband has been getting a little too friendly lately."

"Yes, Mother."

"Any man who can even think of flirting with another woman while his wife is on her deathbed deserves to be shot."

"Can I have seventy-five cents to get my blue dress out of the cleaners?" I asked, though I could tell by the way she was fidgeting with her hairbrush that she was not finished with her own topic.

"Get it out of my pocketbook, and hand me my compact while you're at it." She loosened the knot on her bathrobe and sat down at the kitchen table.

"He calls me out into the hall and asks how his wife is doing, and all the time he's got his hands in his pockets and is giving me this wink. I don't know what he heard about nurses, but I think I set him straight."

I went into the bedroom and started straightening up, hoping she'd stop repeating herself.

"I looked him right in the eye, and I said, 'Mr. Mooney, I think it would be a nice gesture if you went in and held your wife's hand. It might help her forget the pain from her cancer.' "

"I have to leave for school now, Mother," I said, wondering what she'd do if she was taking care of Mr. Pignati. "Give me a kiss."

"Be careful. . . . Lorraine, don't you think that skirt is a little too short?"

"It's the longest skirt in the sophomore class."

"Don't be fresh. Just because all the other girls have sex on their minds, doesn't mean you have to."

John wasn't at the bus stop that morning, but we finally got together during third-period lunch. His hair was combed for the first time in months, and he actually had on a clean shirt. I could tell he was still charged up over our having the Pigman's house to ourselves.

"I didn't get in until the start of the second period."

"How come?"

"Bore wanted to know how I could be missing *forty-two* homework assignments in Problems in American Democracy, and I told him it was because I can't concentrate with the vacuum cleaner going all the time. Then he went off on this big new plan where he's going to check my homework every night, which will last for a day or two until he's too tired or busy."

As he spoke he dragged me to the pay phone in the hall near the principal's office.

"Operator?"

"Yes, sir."

"I just lost my dime trying to get St. Ambrose Hospital. I got some saloon by mistake."

"What number did you want?"

"Sa7-7295."

"I'll ring it for you."

"Thank you, operator." When the hospital answered, John passed the phone to me and stood in the hall to watch for any teachers, because the kids aren't allowed to use the public telephone at Franklin High unless they get a special pass. And even then it's got to be to call your mother to say that the school nurse has just diagnosed leprosy or something.

They gave me the head nurse on Mr. Pignati's floor, and she told me he was going to be in for at least seventy-two hours—the danger period when a lot of people take that second attack and die. She sounded very nice when I told her I was his daughter, and she tried to explain something about this high-voltage machine they've got which is supposed to come in handy if a second attack does come. "Saturday would probably be the earliest he should leave."

"Thank you, ma'am."

"But don't you worry about your father. We're taking very good care of him."

"Thank you."

"As soon as he wakes up from his morning nap I'll tell him you called."

I hung up.

"Is he all right?" John asked.

"Fine." I smiled.

John had the idea it was going to be great fun going over to that house by ourselves, but it didn't work out that way. Monday when we had the spaghetti dinner and put on those costumes was a lovely evening. It really was. I think when we looked at each other in the candlelight, it was the first time

I was glad to be alive. I didn't know exactly why.
It was sort of silly I suppose—him with his moustache
and me with the feather in my hair—but somehow
it was as if I was being told about something, something wonderful, something beautiful waiting just for
me. All I had to do was wait long enough.

Tuesday night I made TV dinners in the oven and
burned them. They were supposed to be pork chops,
but John said they looked like fried dwarf's ears.
Wednesday after school we stopped by the house for
some beer and pretzels, but I knew I wasn't going
to get out that night because my mother was on the
warpath over antifermenting the kitchen. Thursday
we didn't go over there at all because we really
had to go to the library for this report for Problems
in American Democracy:

Read the amendments to the Constitution and condense the
meaning of each into one succinct sentence. Also answer the
following: 1. Which amendment is most important in your
life? 2. Which amendment is least important? 3. What
amendment would you make to the Constitution if you
were President of the United States?

On Friday we cut school since that was the last
day before Mr. Pignati was due home. We got to the
house around eight forty-five in the morning, and
I went right into the kitchen and started making
breakfast. John wanted scrambled eggs with Sloppy-
Joe sauce, and that's what he got. I just had scrambled
eggs with pizza-flavored catsup. I burned the toast
a little, and that was the first of a long list of com-
plaints from Mr. John Conlan.

"*Ohhhhhhhh!*" he groaned.

"I'll put some more bread in."

"It's too late now. My eggs'll get cold."

Then he didn't like my coffee. I tried to explain to him that you can't ruin instant coffee, but he kept insisting I did. I showed him the directions on the label—how you take a level teaspoonful and just add boiling water—but he insisted there was some kind of skill involved.

After breakfast I asked him very nicely to take the garbage out, and he refused.

"Why should I put out the garbage when you're the one who makes it?"

"You make just as much as I do."

"I do not."

"Your beer cans take up most of the space."

"Shut up and do the dishes."

That's the kind of day it started out to be. I wanted to put the place in order so that when Mr. Pignati got back, he wouldn't find a pig house, but the way John was acting I was beginning to feel sorry for his mother if he was always so infantile at home.

"Could *you* do the dishes?" I asked.

"No."

"You could at least do your *own* dishes!"

Every now and then I'm startled at how good-looking John is, but he glared at me from under the shock of hair that fell across his brow and scared me a little. I knew something was bothering him—and I don't mean the dishes or the garbage. If I didn't know how maladjusted John is at times, I would have simply walked out of that house and not spoken to him again as long as I lived. But I let him pout in front of the television and watch a rerun of Doris Day's called *By the Light of the Silvery Moon.*

This particular mood in John had been building up ever since the night that he kissed me in the bedroom. I don't know whether he had just started thinking about our relationship—that I might possibly be something more than his straight man. I really don't know. But suddenly we had become slightly awkward in front of each other. Of course I had always been clumsy around him, but at least I knew I had been in love with him for months. I also knew he liked me a lot but only as a friend or a dreamboat with a leak in it. But now suddenly he was wearing shaving lotion, combing his hair, and fighting with me. There was something about all that which made me smile as I scraped the Sloppy-Joe sauce off his plate.

"I'll take the garbage out now," he said, appearing in the doorway.

"I'd appreciate that very much."

"I'm only doing it because the Pigman's coming home tomorrow, and this hovel better look good."

"Of course."

We really went to work on the house and fixed it up better than ever before. The only room we didn't touch was the one with the pigs in it. There was something almost religious about that room, as though it contained a spirit that belonged only to Mr. Pignati, and it was best left alone.

Once I had a nightmare about that room. I was walking down a long hall and saw the curtains on a doorway at the end. Even though I was dreaming, I knew exactly where I was, and I felt an icy chill run through me. I wanted to run away, but something was pushing me toward the curtains, and I started to scream for John.

"Help me ... help me ... please."

I couldn't stop my legs from moving closer and closer—as if large hands were fastened to them.

The room was very dark though I could make out the shapes of pigs all around me. But instead of being on a table the pigs were arranged on a long black container, and as I started to realize what it was the fingers propelling my legs tightened and moved me closer. I felt the same horrible force taking control of my arms, and I couldn't stop my hands from moving down to the lid of the box. When I touched it my hands went cold, and I knew I was about to open a coffin. I started to cry and plead and call to God to stop me as the lid began to rise.

Then was when I woke up screaming. Right there and then I should have known the dream was an omen of death.

"Lorraine!"

"What's going on in there?" I called from the sofa where I was admiring how clean everything looked. I heard John rummaging through the closets in the kitchen and a banging of bottles. I went to see what he was doing, and he had the kitchen table loaded with all the beer in the house. It wasn't enough to keep the Stork Club in business, but there were a few quarts of beer and some wine.

"John, what are you doing?"

"Is there any more beer in the icebox?"

"What's going on?"

He opened the refrigerator himself and counted about nine loose cans of beer. Then he slammed the door and went into the living room to the telephone.

"We're going to have a few friends over for drinks tonight."

"Are you crazy?"

"Just a few intimate friends for a quiet little drink. Don't you think Mr. Pignati wants us to have a social life?" He smiled, his great big eyes glowing.

13

I really did think Mr. Pignati would have wanted us to have a few friends over. Of course, he would have liked to be there so he wouldn't feel he was missing anything. I knew how much he'd enjoy hearing about a party when he came home. He'd want to know every little detail, just like he asked about everything we did in school.

Dennis came over first around seven thirty because I told him to steal a bottle of 80 proofer out of his father's whiskey cabinet. His father's a building inspector, and everybody who doesn't want to be inspected too much slips him a bottle and a few bucks each month. Dennis also brought some soda mixers and two dozen glasses he got from his mother by telling her I was having a birthday party and they were needed for the lemonade.

I told Dennis not to invite Norton because if there was one thing this little cocktail party didn't need, it was Norton Kelly. Norton has a reputation for going *especially* berserk at parties. Even when we used to have kiddie parties and play spin the bottle, the girls were terrified when it was his turn because he'd bite.

"I don't think we should use all of Mr. Pignati's food," Lorraine said, munching on a saltine.

"He only got the stuff for us."

"He likes snails, so I think we should save all of them for him," she said generously.

Once she started turning out the hors d'oeuvres, she gained momentum. In fact she started eating every other one she made. It was one for the plate and one for her stomach. She put ricotta cheese on crackers, frog's legs on crackers, bamboo shoots on crackers, and fish killies, still with their heads on crackers. The only thing she didn't put on crackers was the chocolate-covered ants, which she just put on a plate so they looked like miniature chocolate candies.

At seven thirty Deanna Deas arrived with her best girl friend Helen Kazinski. The two of them together are known as Beauty and the Beast. Helen is so fat you need a shoehorn to get her in the door. Then a few others arrived: Jane Appling, Rocky Romano, Nick Cahill, James Moon, Marlon Brewery, Josephine Adamo, Tony Remeo, Bernie Iatoni, Barney Friman, and Janice Dickery. They were a real nice bunch, but each one of them had a problem all his own. For instance, Jane Appling is six feet two inches tall.

"Saaaaaay, this is a nice house. Whose is it?" That's the kind of mind Jane has.

"My uncle's," I told her, with just enough hesitation so she'd know I was lying. There's no point in having a house unless kids wonder how you got it. We really didn't start out inviting too many kids, but the more Lorraine and I thought of the parties we had been invited to, the more we had to call. After all, it was the first time either one of us had a chance to return the invitations we had gotten. Lorraine's mother wouldn't allow anybody in her house, and my mother would've insisted on DDT-dusting anyone I wanted to bring home.

Lorraine dragged Jane away from me and over to the telephone while the kids were still quiet and nervous.

"Hello, Mother?" Lorraine started, looking like a thief. "I'm calling from the phone booth at the corner of Jane Appling's block. Her mother just made dinner for us, and I'm going to stay for a couple of hours, and we'll do our homework together."

There was a long silence, and Lorraine's face looked like she was tiptoeing across thin ice. Jane was all set to give her routine because she's the only girl who doesn't have a telephone, so nobody can call back and check out the story.

"Saaaaay, Mrs. Jensen, I really would appreciate it if you'd let Lorraine stay awhile because I don't understand this biology we've got, and your daughter's a real brain."

Most of the kids had been going to a dance down at St. Mary's Hall, but when they heard Lorraine and I were having a party, they ditched that idea. Rocky Romano is the real social organizer of the group. He looks a little bit like a constipated weasel, but he really keeps the party moving. Mainly it's this idiotic face of his.

Nick Cahill's problem is that he's terrified of girls, and Marlon Brewery would be fine if he'd learn how to drink. I mean he reads too much, and he's always worrying about getting liver trouble and things like that. Josephine Adamo is a complete waste not worth mentioning, and Tony Remeo's problem is that he likes opera.

"I think we should save the rest of the ricotta cheese for Mr. Pignati," Lorraine blurted as she went by with a serving tray.

"Miniature chocolates, anyone?"

Barney Friman is the big phony in the group and nobody can stand him, which is the main reason I invited him. Janice Dickery is the only nice one of the first pack. She's really a lovely, sweet girl who dropped out of school in her junior year. I also invited Jack Brahn, but he asked if Janice Dickery was coming. When I said yes, he said no. That was because Jack Brahn was the reason Janice Dickery dropped out of school in her junior year.

The band didn't arrive until much after eight because they had trouble with their amplifiers in the snow. Once they got set up, the house really started to jump. Gary Friman, Barney Friman's brother, played the drums. He was sort of the hero of the teen-age music world ever since he got drunk one night at a party last summer and played the drums in the middle of Victory Boulevard. Billie Baffo was on guitar and Chicken Dee had bass. Melissa Dumas was there too because she goes steady with Gary Friman, and she always sings two songs with the band. She only sings two songs because that's all she knows. She's got a lovely voice, but her memory is like that of a titmouse with curvature of the brain.

Three girls came from the church dance because Jane Appling had invited them, and I think she had one @#$% of a nerve. A few guys crashed with them, and we ended up with not much more than forty or so kids, so—I mean there could have been more—it wasn't bad for a cocktail party.

The chocolate ants and frog' legs were gone in no

time. You can count on kids to eat anything when they're at a party, especially if they don't know it's ants and frogs. And the beer was holding out pretty good. Most of the girls were drinking the wine, but Melissa Dumas had drunk too much. You should've seen her, half loaded, singing:

> Angel, baby . . .
> Myyyyyyyyyy angellllll baaaaaaaaaby,
> It's just like heaaaaaaaaaaaaven . . .
> dreamin' of yaaaaaaa . . .
> armmmmmmmmmmms. . . .

We moved most of the furniture out onto the enclosed porch and took up the rug in the living room, so there was a great dance floor. Janice Dickery did this fantastic shaking that got everybody upset, with only Gary Friman on the drums. Like I told you, she's very mature, and when she shakes, you can understand how come she had to drop out of school in her junior year. Then the guitars came back in, and they had to really show off. They turned the amps up so loud the window panes were rattling.

"The nuns across the street are going to complain," Lorraine yelled to me over the racket.

"Oh shut up," I bellowed back, getting a little high myself, but still rather furious about her telling me I made most of the garbage. I really can't stand it when anyone tells me something like that.

I mean, this was turning out to be the party of the year. The house was a great pleasure palace, it really was. And there wasn't that much damage being done. Somebody dropped a drink down the stairs, and a cigarette burned a small hole in a throw rug.

Only one lamp went over, and that was during this frenzied dance when everybody was on the floor.

> *Angel, baaaaaaaaby . . .*
> *It's just like heaaaaaaaaven. . . .*

I waited until about ten thirty before I put my roller skates on and came tearing onto the dance floor. Melissa Dumas dug Lorraine's pair out of the closet, and she and I did this dance you wouldn't believe.

"Are you enjoying my roller skates?" Lorraine asked.

"I didn't know they were yours," Melissa chirped.

"You never bothered to *ask* either." Lorraine stormed back out to the kitchen, and her face was pink with jealousy.

"Saaaaaay, John" I heard Jane Appling's voice screeching across the room. She was waving her hand like a buxom basketball player. "Where did you *really* get this house?"

Around ten thirty Norton Kelly arrived, and the party was in full swing. He was furious about not being invited—sort of like the witch at Sleeping Beauty's ball. I didn't want any trouble, so I met him at the door.

"Norton, baby, how are you?"

"So you're having a little party, eh?" His mouth twisted like he'd just slammed a car door on his thumb.

"I've tried to get in touch with you all night."

He looked carefully at me to see if I was lying or not. Anyone else would have known I was lying.

"I'll bet you did."

"I did, *really*. Everyone's been wondering where you've been."

"Who?"

"Do you want wine or beer?"

"How could you let that girl use my skates? Tell her to get them off!" Lorraine interrupted, shooting a dirty look at Norton and then dashing off again.

"*Wine.*"

After I took care of him, I went back on the floor and did another skating routine, but I kept watching Norton out of the corner of my eye. He just stood quietly over on one side of the living room, sipping, but you could see him casing the joint like crazy.

"How was I supposed to know they were her skates?" Melissa said, whirling about.

Lorraine looked worried at first when she saw Norton there because she knows how he always goes ape at parties, but eventually she and Helen Kazinski went up to the bedroom to put on some of Conchetta's clothes. Lorraine had the same outfit on she had worn that other night, with the feather in her hair, and Helen Kazinski had this faded yellow dress on, which she couldn't zipper up the back because she's so fat. Helen also found a mangy fur stole that looked like it was made out of four hundred Angora alley cats so, needless to say, she was quite the sight coming down the stairs.

But Lorraine looked beautiful again. Even Melissa was staring at her.

"Don't rip the dress, Helen," Lorraine kept saying.

"I'm not ripping it!"

"I think we'd better take the clothes off, Helen. You're going to ruin that dress."

"Saaaaaay, Lorraine, are there any more Cokes? I need one to wash down those delicious miniature chocolates."

By now the band was blasting like nobody's business, and the usual confusing things happened. Jack Brahn came to the front door and demanded to see Janice Dickery, even though he refused to come in. Melissa Dumas and Chicken Dee, who plays bass, were making out on the porch, and she still had the roller skates on. If Gary Friman, who goes steady with Melissa Dumas, ever found out, there'd be blood on the floor.

About a half hour after Norton arrived, I noticed he had disappeared. I skated through the downstairs, and then I got a little worried. I mean, like I said, he's the type of psycho who'd set a house on fire if he felt like it.

"Did you see Norton?" I yelled to Lorraine, who was running around emptying ashtrays.

"I saw him go upstairs," she called back, blowing a strand of hair away from her face.

I went up with my skates still on—*clomp! clomp! clomp!*—and Deanna Deas and Janice Dickery were rushing down in costume.

> . . . *just like heeeeeeaven* . . .
> *dreeeeeeamin' here with*
> *yoooooooooouuuuuuuuuuu.* . . .

My heart started pounding like crazy because I knew if I found what I thought I would, I'd really blow my lid. At the top I opened the door on the left, and sure enough there was good old Norton putting the guts of this junky old oscilloscope back in its case and getting ready to cart it out of the house.

"Hi there, Johnny-boy," he said. Then he broke into

a little smile as he went on with what he was doing.

"Leave it alone."

"Leave what alone?"

I tensed, ready to punch him.

"Oh, you don't want to be rude to your friends, Johnny-boy, now do you? Share and share alike."

"I don't have any Marshmallow Kids for friends, you 3@‡$%!"

"John!" I heard Lorraine yell from the foot of the stairs, and the split second in which I turned my head gave Norton the chance he was waiting for. He drove his fist into my stomach and knocked the wind out of me. I don't think I would have fallen down if I hadn't been wearing the roller skates, but Norton just picked up the oscilloscope and beat it. It was a piece of garbage, and if that got him out of the house, I would have felt lucky. But when I got to the top of the stairs, I saw him ducking through the crowd toward the back of the house.

Angel baaaaaaby . . . baaaaaby angel. . . .

I clomped down the stairs, which were draped with bodies by this time. The band was still clanging away, and Lorraine was motioning like she was going to drop from fright.

"There's a car outside, John. I think it's a taxi!"

I remember thinking that it couldn't be the Pigman. He wouldn't be coming home at night. He wasn't the type who would get a crazy idea like just checking out and coming back to us and his pigs because he didn't feel like spending another night in the hospital. They wouldn't have let him, I thought. Of course not.

When I got into the dining room, I heard the sound of things breaking. The noise was coming from the room with the black curtains. The pig room.

"John!" Lorraine screamed. "Someone's coming up the front steps!"

I pushed the curtains open, and there was Norton holding a large white pig, which he brought down suddenly on a table edge, knocking its head off. He looked inside and then threw it against the wall where it blasted to pieces. Several other broken pigs were laying all over the floor, and the only thing I could think of at that moment was the proud and happy look on Mr. Pignati's face when he had shown us the pigs that first day. I felt like killing Norton as I plowed into him, punching his face like it was a sack of flour. After I got a couple of good blows in, he dug his elbow into my ribs and kicked the skates out from under me. That gave him a chance to pick up the oscilloscope and head for the door like a scared rat.

I went racing out of the room and noticed the band had stopped playing. I knew the place was emptying, and suddenly I realized what Lorraine was saying.

"The Pigman's here!"

A second later my hands grabbed the back of Norton's neck, and I pushed him forward with so much force he must have traveled the length of the living room before we both fell to the floor. The oscilloscope shattered right near the front hallway, and when I saw the blood pouring out of Norton's nose, I was so happy I began to laugh. But then it was quiet.

Finally I managed to lift my head and saw Mr.

Pignati at the door. He was just standing there looking down at me, and there was no smile on his face. No smile at all.

That's when I passed out.

14

A policeman with a beer belly helped me get John into the patrol car—roller skates and all. Two nuns were walking on the other side of the street, and they watched us so closely one of them almost fell on the ice.

"You're just lucky the old guy isn't going to press charges," the cop said, practically slamming the door on John's foot and then getting into the driver's seat. I tried to get John to come alive, but he was motionless in the back seat next to me. The police had pulled up just as I was getting him off the floor, and everyone else had gotten away.

"Okay, let's go," the other policeman said, coming out of the house and getting into the front. He was so much taller and thinner than the other one that the two of them together looked rather incongruous.

"Is Mr. Pignati all right?" I asked. The last I had seen of him was when he climbed the stairs with one of Conchetta's dresses over his arm—the one Helen Kazinski had ripped—and I just didn't know what to say to him.

"Could you let me see him a minute?"

"No, he's upstairs—"

"Is he all right?"

"He's crying, if you really want to know. The old guy's crying."

I sank back in the seat and started to tremble. It was cold and I didn't have a coat, but I wasn't shaking just because of that. I tried to pinch John so he'd come to, but it was no use.

"John, wake up!"

"He's out for the night," the fat cop said, adjusting his hat.

"I want to see what kind of parents you kids have," the skinny one added, lighting a cigarette and blowing the smoke into the back seat. "Do they know you go over to that old man's house? We've seen you hanging around there before."

I looked at John crumpled and twisted in the corner, the roller skates pointing every which way. I couldn't find his shoes or my clothes in the excitement—and somehow the laces on his skates had knotted and frozen so I couldn't untie them anyway. The thought of my mother seeing me in the ruffled dress terrified me, and I hated John at that moment for having gotten me into this. I hated him more for being drunk when I needed him.

"This where you live?"

"Yes . . . please. . . ."

"Do you kids always get your kicks picking on old people?"

"Please just let us go. I promise we won't do anything like this again. We won't go over there anymore." I was ashamed of myself because I was beginning to plead.

"Let's just talk to your family a minute," the skinny one said, opening his door. I burst into tears as the cold air rushed into the car.

"Not one cent for tribute!" John suddenly mumbled, leaning forward, laughing, and then falling back unable to hold his head up. He was hopelessly drunk, and I slammed the door of the patrol car. The policeman took me up the steps.

"My mother's going to beat me."

"You should've thought about that a little earlier, young lady." He rang the bell.

I knew it would take a minute while she peered out one of the front windows, realized who it was, and then put on a bathrobe. When I heard her footsteps coming, my heart seemed to be beating in time with them until the door opened.

"Where are your clothes, Lorraine?" was the first thing she said, standing in the shadow of the doorway, looking at the policeman and me. Her hair was down, and she pulled the blue robe tight around her.

"This your daughter, ma'am?"

"What's the matter?"

"She and a few of her friends had too much to drink tonight at some old man's house on Howard Avenue. They almost wrecked the place."

I couldn't look at her, and as soon as my eyes went down she knew I was guilty.

"Where are your clothes, Lorraine?" she repeated slowly, reaching her hands out for my shoulders. She pulled me closer to her. "Look at me, Lorraine."

Her eyes burned into me.

"What are you doing in this dress?"

I opened my mouth and tried to get the words out but couldn't speak. Tears began to roll down my cheeks, and she raised her hand and slapped me.

"No, Mother," I screamed, and even the policeman

jumped and looked sorry he had brought me to the door.

"Get inside," she ordered, and her voice had switched from the hysterical to the commanding, like I'd often heard it do when she was working as a nurse. She always had the ability to deal with doctors and policemen if she was forced to.

I had just enough time to get out of the dress, wash the smeared makeup off my face, and put on a pair of pajamas before I heard the front door slam—which I knew was for my benefit. A moment later she was in the doorway, looking at me, the expression on her face somewhere between disbelief and disgust.

"I didn't do anything wrong," I said slowly, unsure of what her next move would be. I wanted to scream the thoughts that were flashing through my mind at her. I wanted to tell her how she didn't know anything about me—how she hadn't noticed that I happened to be a human being myself . . . that I wasn't still the little girl that waved from the window when she stood at a bus stop. Look at me, I wanted to yell, can't you see I'm growing up and that I've got to have friends? That I *want* to have friends—that I need other people in this world besides you!

She came toward me, and I backed away until I was cornered by the wall. Then she raised her arm and slapped me once more across the face. She tried to hit me again, but my arm went up and blocked her.

"You lied to me."

"I didn't mean to."

"You lied."

"It was only a party. You wouldn't have let me go."

She broke down crying and turned away, putting her hands up to her face, and I knew she wanted me to run after her to beg forgiveness. I *won't*, I thought. For the first time in my life I'm not going to. It's the Pigman who has to forgive me—not you!

She was sitting at the kitchen table, crying—a slightly exaggerated crying which seemed to make our relationship even more artificial.

You're the one who's wrong, I wanted to tell her, not me.

Then I remembered all the times I had wakened up years ago. I'd wake up, and she wouldn't know it—and I'd get out of bed and peek in the kitchen. Sometimes I'd be able to see through the keyhole or a crack in the door, and she'd be sitting at the table, crying. But I wasn't supposed to hear it then.

"Mother?"

Her crying lowered just a little, and I went to the table and hugged her.

"I've tried to do the best I could . . . I've worked night and day to keep a roof over our heads . . . you think it's easy raising a kid by yourself. . . ."

Once that stage was over, I began slowly to explain to her what I'd been up to—Mr. Pignati and John and me. Of course, I edited it considerably for her benefit, and she seemed to take it well, now that the emotional raving was over. There were a few moments of minor relapses, like when I told her I had never belonged to the Latin Club, but on the whole she took things better than I thought she would.

Finally we went to bed, and just as I was feeling better because I had been relatively honest with her, just as I started to think she understood a little and recognized that she had given birth to a human being with a normal-sized brain, I heard this voice in my ear: "You're sure the old man didn't try anything with you?"

"What?" I mumbled, not turning toward her.

"*Sexually*," she whispered.

"No, Mother."

"Those old men have ways, Lorraine. Sometimes they touch you, and you may not even notice what they're doing."

"Good night, Mother," I said, rearranging myself with finality, knowing that she could never really understand.

I felt tears rolling down my cheeks onto the pillow as I remembered the condition of Mr. Pignati's house. Would he think we had forsaken him and deliberately ripped his wife's clothes—viciously broken the pigs? I wanted to phone him and say, Mr. Pignati, we didn't mean things to work out like that. We were just playing.

Playing.

Play.

I couldn't get the word out of my mind. I remembered a cat playing with a rubber ball somewhere . . . a kitten a girl friend had gotten for her birthday . . . and it was hiding behind a chair leg eyeing the ball . . . stalking it. The kitten knew what it was because it had been toying with it all along, but now it attacked, claws drawn, trying to sink its teeth into the soft rubber.

"Look at the kitty playing with the ball," the girl's mother had said.

The cat attacked the ball as if it were a living

thing. I remember thinking it was practicing for when it might have to kill to survive. *Play* was something natural, I remember thinking—something which Nature wanted us to do to prepare us for later life.

"I am a handsome European businessman, and you are in love with me!"

"Stop it, John."

"Come to me, my darling, one kiss is all I ask!"

"Please stop. . . ."

"You look beautiful!"

"Do you mean it?"

A boy with a moustache, a girl with a feather.

Then I fell asleep.

"Lorraine" I heard my mother call. I opened my eyes just enough to see her standing over me in her white uniform. The morning light was painful.

"Those nylon stockings you brought home—"

"What about them?"

"You didn't do anything *bad* for them, did you?"

"No, Mother," I said, burying my head in the pillow and wondering at just what point that little thought had come to her. She came in and out of the bedroom several times, and I pretended to be asleep. Just before she left for work she said loudly, "Don't think I'm through with you yet. You get this house cleaned up, and I'll want to talk to you when I get home."

John gave the one-ring signal about eleven o'clock, which was much earlier than I had expected because I thought he'd still be unconscious. We met at the corner. He looked very disheartened.

"My father says I have to go to a psychiatrist."

"He'll forget about it in a day or two," I reminded him.

"I know."

We walked down Victory Boulevard toward Tony's Market because he wanted a pack of cigarettes. Josephine Adamo passed on the other side of the street, and she yelled, "Some party!" She had left before the fight, and you could tell by the expression on her face that she hadn't heard about it yet.

"What did they do when the police brought you to the door?" I asked.

John picked up a handful of slush and started molding it into an iceball.

"My mother started her high-frequency cackling, but it was Bore who got on my nerves. He just came to the top of the stairs, and I could hardly hold my head up to see him. My mother was on her hands and knees, wiping up the snow I dragged in on the skates. Bore didn't even look mad. He looked sick and old. Then he went back into the bedroom without a word. This morning at breakfast he said they'd have to send me to a doctor."

He threw the iceball at a telephone pole, but it missed and hit a parked car.

"Was Mr. Pignati all right?" he asked sheepishly.

"What do you care?" I said with an edge to my voice so he'd know I blamed everything on him. Then I was sorry I'd said it.

"I just wondered," he said, looking away and raising his eyes to the sky where a jet was roaring over. We finally got to the store and stood by the telephone booth having a Coke. John smoked a second cigarette, and then somehow we got enough nerve.

"Hello, Mr. Pignati?"

There was a long pause, although you could tell somebody had answered.

"Mr. Pignati, this is John."

There was an even longer pause, and the artificial enthusiasm John had put into his voice trailed off. "Are you there, Mr. Pignati?"

"Yes—" came this weak voice.

"Lorraine and I want to apologize for having that party. We had only invited two people, but those others stopped by, and before you knew it things got out of hand. I mean, Lorraine and I will pay for everything."

I gasped audibly.

John started again. "Are you still there, Mr. Pignati?"

"Yes."

"Would you let Lorraine and me come over to help clean up? Please?"

"No ... it's all right. ..."

"Mr. Pignati, we feel terrible," I said into the mouthpiece and then handed it back to John. I felt on the verge of crying, thinking of the broken pigs.

"Mr. Pignati, we'd really feel better if—"

"I cleaned most of it," he said slowly.

"Mr. Pignati, are you there?"

There was another pause.

"Yes. ..."

"Lorraine and I want to know if you'd like to go to the zoo this afternoon. We thought we could meet you around one o'clock near the entrance. You know, right by the sea lions?"

Another pause.

"We could go and feed Bobo," John said. "Have you been down to see Bobo yet?"

Another pause.

"No. ..."

"He must miss you, Mr. Pignati. No kidding. The

way you used to feed him every day. What do you say, Mr. Pignati?"

As we waited for an answer all I could think of was Conchetta's ripped dress—the one Helen Kazinski had demolished. It must have been a shock to come home from the hospital and find something like that.

"All right . . ." Mr. Pignati said sadly.

We got to the zoo around twelve thirty, and I didn't think the Pigman was going to show. I really didn't. We sat on the same bench as we had last time, the one near the front gate that lets you watch the sea lions. I had my Ben Franklin sunglasses on again, and it wasn't even sunny out, but I figured they'd be good because I wouldn't have to look right into anyone's eyes. One of the attendants was washing the sea-lion manure off the middle platform of the pool, and at least he was able to do that with a certain degree of proficiency. When it came to feeding them he had no imagination, but that particular task he was up to.

"He's not coming," I said when it was five minutes past one.

"Just wait. He'll be here."

No customers were over by the peanut stand where that same old woman from the last visit was giving me the evil eye. Worst of all, she was putting peanuts into her mouth at the same rate Jane Appling had devoured the chocolate-covered ants. She really looked like the wrath of God, and I was too scared to go over and buy a package of peanuts for myself.

"I'll get some peanuts for Bobo," John said.

"And me!" I yelled after him.

About ten minutes later a taxi pulled up in front,

and the Pigman got out. There was no smile on his face. He walked very slowly, and he had lost so much weight. It was pathetic, that's what it was. Absolutely pathetic.

"Hello," John said cheerfully, covering his own surprise at the change in the Pigman's appearance.

"Hello," Mr. Pignati said, forcing a slight smile. You could tell he was glad to see us, but I knew he was very sick. He certainly had forgiven us for anything we did over at the house or else he wouldn't have come—so I figured he was just weak from his heart attack and the hospital. Naturally we decided to take the train-type contraption out to the monkey house.

"I bought peanuts for Bobo," John said, proudly waving the bags. I had already started eating mine.

"I have some . . . money," Mr. Pignati said, reaching a hand into one of his pockets.

"I have it, Mr. Pignati," John insisted, giving a dollar bill to the man in the ticket booth.

We squeezed into the last car, and the same blond boy was driving again. There was quite a wind even though it had warmed up enough to start the snow melting, and it made the frilly canopy on the cars snap loudly. We didn't say anything more—Mr. Pignati wedged right between us—as we rolled along the bleak pathways of the zoo.

We went by the bald eagle, the white-tailed deer, the tahr goats, the lions, and the striped hyena. They all seemed to be frozen—giant stuffed animals, unable to move. Then came the tigers and bears, the two hippos who were inside for the season, and the eight-ton bull elephant, the only part of which we could see being the long trunk protruding from the doorway of his barn. Even the alligator pond had been drained.

"Bobo will be glad to see you," John said finally.

Nobody answered.

We pulled the buzzer for the guy to stop the contraption at the primate house, and John had to help Mr. Pignati get off.

"Easy now, Mr. Pignati."

"Thank you." The Pigman smiled, and you could tell he was anxious to see his baboon.

"Bobo's going to be so happy to see you," I said, trying for another smile.

All the outside portion of the monkey house was closed, so we went inside, and it was obvious that even in the winter those apes desperately need deodorant pads. Even Limburger-cheese spray would've been an improvement.

We started walking down the long chamber with all the cages on both sides, and the only other people there were an attendant hosing out the gorilla cage and some woman holding a two-year-old baby.

I stopped and watched the man at the gorilla cage while Mr. Pignati and John went on to the next one, which was Bobo's. Right away I noticed something was wrong because the two of them started getting nervous and looking all around the place. Mr. Pignati went up to the rail and started calling, "Bobo? Bobo?"

The man cleaning the gorilla cage shut off the water and started to roll up the hose when he heard Mr. Pignati calling. I moved up and could see the cage was completely empty, but I thought they had just moved the baboon to some other cage. I knew he wasn't on the outside part because it was too cold.

"Bobo? Bobo?"

"Bobo died last week," the attendant said, still rolling up the hose.

"The baboon?" John asked.

"Yep. Can't say I felt particularly sorry about it because that baboon had the nastiest disposition around here." The attendant wiped his nose on his sleeve and continued rolling up the hose. "Did an autopsy on him, and it looked like pneumonia."

Mr. Pignati kept staring into the cage, and we stood motionless for what seemed like an eternity.

"Mr. Pignati," John said softly, "we'd better leave."

"Bobo. . . ."

I could see the blood vessels on the side of Mr. Pignati's neck pulse as he raised his right hand to his face. I was thankful I had my sunglasses on because I didn't want to see his eyes. I mean, I just didn't. Even John just stood there not knowing what to do.

"Had a Woolly monkey down the end that died from pneumonia too," the attendant muttered, almost to himself.

As I started moving away and heading for the door John went to Mr. Pignati and just took his arm lightly, trying to turn him away from the empty cage. I saw the Pigman open his mouth, and then his hands started to shake. He went to grab hold of the railing, but let out a tiny cry almost like a puppy that had been stepped on by mistake. I can still remember the sound of it, and sometimes I wake up from a nightmare with it in my ears. It was like a high-pitched scream, but it came from deep inside of him, and before John or I knew what had happened, the Pigman dropped to the floor. It seemed as if the monkeys knew something had happened because they started making noise and pulling against the bars. I thought they were going to tear them out of the frames, and I wanted to put my hands to my ears to shut out the jungle that had surrounded us.

Mr. Pignati was dead.

15

"What happened?" the attendant asked in a scared, dumb voice.

"Call an ambulance!" I yelled. He looked at me for a moment as though what I said was too complicated to understand, and then he was off.

"You'd better get out of here," I said to Lorraine. When I touched her she burst into tears and ran out of the monkey house. If she had gotten involved as a witness after all that had happened, I knew her mother would've shipped her off to a Tibetan convent for ninety-six years.

The lady with the baby in her arms just sneaked out a door. You could tell her motto was "When trouble strikes—vanish." Then it was just me on my knees next to Mr. Pignati, and just as suddenly as the monkeys had started screaming they shut up. One tiny monkey with yellow frames around his eyes pressed against the bars of his cage to watch me take the Pigman's wrist. I felt for a pulse, but there was nothing. Lorraine had dropped her sunglasses, so I crawled the short distance over to them and back to Mr. Pignati's side. When I held one of the glass ovals near his mouth, there was no breath to cloud the surface.

Did you have to die? I wanted to bend down and whisper in his ear. They say when you die your brain lives for awhile longer, and maybe he could've heard me.

A small trickle of saliva had started from the corner of his mouth, and I placed my handkerchief against it and turned his head slightly. What would there be to say even if he could've heard me?

"Is Mr. Pignati all right?"

"What do you care?" Lorraine had said that morning.

But I did care. She thinks she knows everything that goes on inside me, and she doesn't know a thing. What did she want from me—to tell the truth all the time? To run around saying it did matter to me that I live in a world where you can grow old and be alone and have to get down on your hands and knees and beg for friends? A place where people just sort of forget about you because you get a little old and your mind's a bit senile or silly? Did she think that didn't bother me underneath? That I didn't know if we hadn't come along the Pigman would've just lived like a vegetable until he died alone in that dump of a house?

"Do you think you'd like to go to the zoo with me tomorrow, Mr. Wandermeyer and Miss Truman.

"Please. . . ."

"Please."

Didn't she know how sick to my stomach it made me feel to know it's possible to end your life with only a baboon to talk to? And maybe Lorraine and I were only a different kind of baboon in a way. Maybe we were all baboons for that matter—big blabbing baboons—smiling away and not really caring what was going on as long as there were enough peanuts bouncing around to think about—the whole pack of us—Bore and the Old Lady and Lorraine's mother included—baffled baboons concentrating on all the wrong things.

Everything was so screwed up.

"Your problem is you've got too much spare time."

That was the secret—don't have any spare time. Watch the little things in life, the ones you have control over. Keep your eyes glued to the peas and every speck of dust on the floor.

"Kenneth is doing very nicely."

To @‡$% with Kenneth. To @‡$% with marching along with an attaché case swinging in the breeze.

The tile floor was cold and uncomfortable, and the attendant had dripped some water near me. As I stood up, a hundred thoughts raced through my mind at the same time, one of which was to check Mr. Pignati's wallet to make sure the police could identify him when they got there. Then I wouldn't have to get involved at all. I was ashamed of thinking about myself, though actually it was Bore that I was thinking of now. The position of Mr. Pignati's head on the floor made his face look a little like my father's, and I didn't like the feeling it gave me. Up until then I had never been particularly disturbed about seeing a corpse—even when I'd have to sit for an hour or so at a funeral parlor when some relative had died. To me the dead body just looked like a doll, and all the flowers stuffed around here and there were sort of nice. It gave me a feeling like being in Beekman's toy department to tell the truth—everything elaborately displayed. So many things to look at. Anything to get away from what was really happening.

I lit a cigarette and watched the smoke climb

toward a light in the ceiling. There was such a chill in me I couldn't stop my legs from shaking, and although I was standing in the same spot, I felt as if I were moving forward. My thoughts jumped from Mr. Pignati to wondering if Lorraine were waiting for me, to knowing I was standing in a monkey house stuck on top of a small planet whirling through space. Moving forward. It was like Lorraine's nightmare, where something forced her toward the room with the black curtains.

Then I knew.

I was not in a monkey house. For a moment it was something else—something I was glimpsing for the first time—the cold tiles, the draft that moved about me, the nice solid fact that someday I was going to end up in a coffin myself.

My tomb.

I took a puff on the cigarette, and I could hear Lorraine's voice saying I was killing myself. As if I didn't know it! Did she think I thought smoking and drinking were supposed to make me live longer? I knew what it was doing to me.

"You must want to die," she had said once, and maybe that was true. Maybe I would rather be dead than to turn into the kind of grown-up people I knew. What was so hot about living anyway if people think you're a disturbing influence just because you still think about God and Death and the Universe and Love. My poor mother and father—I wanted to tell them that they no longer wonder what they're doing in the world while I stand here going out of my mind.

I stayed until the ambulance doctor gestured that the Pigman was dead. A whole crowd of people had gathered to crane their necks and watch them roll a

dead man onto a stretcher. I don't know where they
all came from so quickly. It must have been announced over the loudspeaker. Hey everybody! Come
see the dead man in the monkey house. Step right up.
Special feature today.

"Good-bye, Mr. Pignati," I said, hardly moving my
lips. The police and attendants moved calmly, surely,
as if they were performing a ritual and had forgotten
the meaning of it. I don't think they ever *knew* the
meaning of it. I thought of machinery—automatic,
constant, unable to be stopped.

The sun had come out, and I had to cover my
eyes. Finally I saw Lorraine sitting on a bench in
the large center mall near the entrance of the zoo.
There was a long pond that was heated in some way
so the water wouldn't freeze and kill the fish, and
she looked strange surrounded by the mist that rose
from its surface.

"Here's your glasses."

She didn't answer at first—just kept looking at the
ground. Then she struck out at me, as though trying
to punch me.

"We murdered him," she screamed, and I turned
away because I had been through just about all I
could stand.

"Here's your glasses," I said again, almost hating her
for a second. I wanted to yell at her, tell her he had
no business fooling around with kids. I wanted to tell
her he had no right going backward. When you grow
up, you're not supposed to go back. Trespassing—
that's what he had done.

I sat down next to her and lit up another cigarette.
I couldn't help but look at the flashing light on top
of the ambulance. They had driven it right up to the
entrance of the monkey house, and it looked weird

because it didn't belong. Right in the bright sunlight you could see the flashing dome going like crazy, pulsing like a heartbeat.

Then I saw this ridiculous sight running toward us from the other end of the mall—a great big fat man in a stupid-looking uniform, clutching a fistful of strings attached to helium balloons that bobbed in the air behind him. He was hobbling as fast as he could go, right toward the monkey house, with this sign around his neck: *BUY YOUR FUNNY-FACE BALLOONS HERE!*

Lorraine lifted her head slightly and watched him go by. Then she broke down crying again and turned away so she was facing the pond and didn't have to look at me. I noticed a whole school of goldfish practically sticking their noses out of the water because they thought someone was going to feed them. In the deep center a large carp flipped its tail and then disappeared as quickly as it had surfaced.

"Let's go, Lorraine," I said softly, standing beside her. I lowered the sunglasses, and she took them, almost dropping them again trying to get them on.

Her hand lingered near mine, and I took it gently. She seemed funny peering up at me over the thin metal rims. We looked at each other. There was no need to smile or tell a joke or run for roller skates. Without a word, I think we both understood.

We had trespassed too—been where we didn't belong, and we were being punished for it. Mr. Pignati had paid with his life. But when he died something in us had died as well.

There was no one else to blame anymore. No Bores or Old Ladies or Nortons, or Assassins waiting at the bridge. And there was no place to hide—no place across any river for a boatman to take us.

Our life would be what we made of it—nothing more, nothing less.

Baboons.

Baboons.

They build their own cages, we could almost hear the Pigman whisper, as he took his children with him.

ABOUT THE AUTHOR

PAUL ZINDEL is the author of seven novels for young adults, a picture book, four theater plays and numerous screenplays. He has an M.S. in education and has received an honorary doctorate from Wagner College. For ten years he was a high school chemistry teacher on his native Staten Island, New York, and then was awarded a Ford Foundation grant as writer-in-residence at Nina Vance's Alley Theater in Houston, Texas.

He enjoys television, movies, dream interpretation, swimming and all fattening foods—particularly Hunan cuisine and ice cream. He also likes new experiences (he's currently trying his hand at acting) and teenagers who need someone to confide in.

A PERSONAL NOTE
by Paul Zindel

One of the most enjoyable things about having written *The Pigman* is the mail I get from kids who have read the book, and I thought you might be interested in reading a few of my favorite letters. (If you feel like writing a letter of your own, my address is below and I'd love to hear from you!) I'm also going to respond to some of the most frequently asked questions from kids around the country about *The Pigman*, but first a few of the letters:

Dear Mr. Zindel: I thoroughly enjoyed *The Pigman* and your other books. I hope that in the future your novels remain of the same high quality because the characters in them are as interesting and whacko as I am! Sincerely, Brian from Ft. Lauderdale.

Dear Mr. Zindel: I think *The Pigman* hit home with a lot of young teenagers today simply because it is about two normal teenagers having a ball, and getting into a little bit of trouble. Your novel speaks to me personally because it's the other side of the street. I don't drink or smoke or my father would tie me in bubble gum, blow me up, and snap me. Yours truly, Mike, Minn.

153

And my favorite letter of all time might very well be from a girl named Kathie who lives in Tulsa, Oklahoma:

Dear Mr. Zindel: When you feel something very deeply it is often times difficult to say exactly what is rattling around in your brain. "Ah ha!" you say, "An insane teenager has written to me!" You might be right. When I finished reading *The Pigman* it pulled a part of me out and I want to finish this letter before that part of me goes back in. I am still not quite in grip of my senses. I'm very spaced out which usually means I'm in top form. I wanted to cry so badly when the Pigman died that it hurt. But something inside me refused to let tears run down my cheeks. I know two kids like John and Lorraine, and I know how terrible they must have felt—but my friends never learned a lesson from their experiences. I cried too many times for them and I guess that's why I didn't have any tears left for your characters. I am too young to understand how anyone can write a book as perceptive as yours but it had a part of almost everyone I know in it, and I can't be sure which one was me. I am very moved. I am speechless. I want you to know that, Mr. Zindel.

Anyway, those are a few of my more interesting letters and I didn't put them in to pat myself on the back but to urge any other kids who feel like writing me to please be very free and open and don't worry about your spelling or grammar and things like that. I'm most interested in your ideas, but I also love hearing about your dreams and just about anything you care to tell me straight from your heart.

Now here are a few questions I often get asked:

WHAT INSPIRED YOU TO WRITE *THE PIGMAN*?

I was living in a fifty-room haunted ex-convent when a boy by the name of John came across the side lawn and I went out to yell at him for trespassing. He was ready to sock me, but instead we decided to talk things out, and it turned out he was a fascinating fifteen year old with parents, teachers, and truant officers who never took the time to understand him. He also drank a lot of beer and had a girlfriend who used to cry anytime anything to do with war was mentioned because she knew someone who had been shot and killed.

HOW DID YOU DECIDE TO HAVE A CHARACTER WHO COLLECTS PIGS?

An actor in Houston, Texas, invited me over for dinner one night and cooked a poached fish which tasted horrible—but he told me he once knew a man from Boston who collected piggybanks, and I never forgot that fact. I always wondered what kind of man would collect piggybanks.

WHERE DID YOU GET THE STORY ABOUT THE BOATMAN?

I got it from the famous playwright Edward Albee who told me about it the night he and I had a meal together. He told me he learned it in Greece.

DID YOU HAVE ANY FUN WRITING THE BOOK?

Yes! The most fun I had was making up names for some of the people at the party. I made the names similar to those of my friends and enemies and changed them just enough.

ARE THE FEELINGS OF THE CHARACTERS YOUR FEEL-INGS?

Yes. For the most part. A novel if it is totally honest is like a dream. One of the most amazing things you learn about dreams is that each person and thing in your dream is an extension of your emotional self. In our dreams we are man, woman, child, animal, and object.

HOW DID YOU GET THE FEELINGS OF YOUR CHARACTERS INTO YOUR WRITING OF *THE PIGMAN*?

I sat around and daydreamed a lot and waited for memories to come. If I needed Norton to do something mean, I just remembered when I did something mean like putting glue in my mother's lock on her telephone. If I needed a character to feel love for another, I tried to remember what it ws like when I was fifteen and felt love. I only used specks of reality, and the source of these specks came from myself, other people, newspapers, magazines, TV, parents, teachers, librarians, and kids. I talked to lots and lots of kids and took notes.

WAS LORRAINE'S MOTHER A REAL PERSON?

She was based on my mother. My mother had a nice side too, but I didn't seem to choose to write about that part in the book.

WHY DID YOU LET THE PIGMAN DIE?

The story just seemed to point that way, but remember what I said in answer to another question about all the emotions being based inside me to some extent? On some level I'm afraid of death and by having a character I created die, I felt death might somehow be less frightening to me.

WHAT DO YOU THINK WOULD HAVE HAPPENED TO JOHN AND LORRAINE AFTER THEY GOT OLDER?

I'm writing about that in a new book called *The*

Pigman Returns. All I know so far is it's not about a ghost.

HOW MUCH MONEY DID YOU MAKE ON THE BOOK?

Considering all rights, movie options, subsidiary deals, etc.—about half a million dollars. The government takes most of it. Others, like agents, get some. But there's still enough left over to eat with and buy toys for my kids who are absolutely wild. They spend most of the day trying to knock each other off. But, beyond the money I do love to write, and if a teacher (or you?) thinks you should be a writer, give it some serious thought. It's a wonderful profession.

WHY DO YOU ALWAYS USE SO MANY SCHOOL REFERENCES?

Because kids feel strongly about school, one way or the other—and it helps create a sense of reality for my stories. I prefer real kids, not kids on the moon.

WHY DO THE CHARACTERS' PARENTS ALWAYS HAVE SUCH SMALL ROLES AND WHY ARE THEY SOMETIMES MEAN?

Because kids don't like to admit how strong an influence parents have on them, and it's natural to have to reject them to some extent in order to find themselves. Otherwise kids would end up being exactly like their parents, and the world wouldn't move forward. There's plenty of time later on in life for most kids to come back to their parents and cherish and appreciate them, if they deserve it.

WHY DO YOU USE SUCH SUPERCHARGED LANGUAGE?

I've tried to use the language of kids, which I find particularly "delicious."

WHAT ARE OTHER INGREDIENTS YOU CONSIDER IMPORTANT FOR A YOUNG ADULT BOOK?

Romance, honesty, mischief, action, and suspense. The same ingredients for any book.

HOW DID YOU FIRST GET A NOVEL PUBLISHED?

Charlotte Zolotow, an editor at Harper & Row and author of picture books, was watching a TV version of my play *The Effect of Gamma Rays on Man-in-the-Moon Marigolds* starring Eileen Heckart, and was moved to write me a letter asking if there were any stories I'd like to write as a novel for young people. I wrote back quickly—yep! I had been a chemistry teacher for ten years and had a million stories! I then wrote *The Pigman*.

DO YOU THINK YOUNG ADULT BOOKS CAN BE USED TO IMPROVE THE LIVES OF YOUNG PEOPLE?

Yes. When a writer creates a book he freezes certain observations about life into words and what I find most exciting and valuable about reading is when you can relate the book back to your own experience. When you can say: 1.) *Hey, I understand what these words say, that John Conlan sat across from his girlfriend and they had secrets to share over a candlelit dinner they concocted;* 2.) *And hey, I think I would have done something else if I was left alone in a house with a girl like that. I would have behaved differently here and the same as John at another point;* 3.) *And hey, this event reminds me of the time I was alone with a girl in a cemetery and we told each other we heard footsteps and thought we saw a hand reach out of a grave!*
These are the ways reading can enrich your life and this is what I feel reading is all about.

Paul Zindel
1156 Eventide Place
Beverly Hills, CA 90210

"I love the school cafeteria in fifth period because there's a girl in there with long, straight, black hair, whose name is Edna Shinglebox, and she looks as freaky and depressed as I am."

Marsh Mellow in PARDON ME, YOU'RE STEPPING ON MY EYEBALL!

"Since lunch I went to the gym and cut 7th period. I'm sending you this via Helen Mackey if she goes to your 9th. Just had to tell you they started doing wheelbarrows in gym. I refused! I told the looney teacher I was under the care of a chiropractor and he said wheelbarrows weren't good for me. Have you seen Sean? He hasn't called me all week. I don't care. If you see him, make sure you tell him I don't care."

Liz Carstensen's note in MY DARLING, MY HAMBURGER

"I don't really know what I'm going to do. It's not going to be that Love Land crap. And I'm not going to give civilization a kick in the behind, because I might need an appendectomy sometime. But I'm going to do something, and I have a strange feeling it's going to be phantasmagorically different."

Dewey Daniels in I NEVER LOVED YOUR MIND

"My name is Christopher. My friends would call me Chris, but I don't have any friends. No real friends. I also have no father. Now, once upon a time I did have a father and my father and Helen really loved each other very much for the first seven years they were married, and then after that they hated each other so much that my father pulled that old trick of saying he was going out to buy the evening paper but went to Mexico."

Christopher Boyd in CONFESSIONS OF A TEENAGE BABOON

These are a few of the many voices created by Paul Zindel in his popular novels that have become worldwide favorites. In addition to the above books, his successful works include THE PIGMAN and the Pulitzer Prize-winning play, THE EFFECT OF GAMMA RAYS ON MAN-IN-THE-MOON MARIGOLDS. His stories are about loners, with bad complexions, goofy parents and startling problems.

Zindel's books reflect teenage living—both the joys and the pains. As he says, "Teenagers feel they are misfits. They're at an age when they should feel out of place. It's a natural condition. I know it's a continuing battle to get through the years between twelve and twenty, so I always write from the teenager's point of view."

Zindel's own early years were difficult. Besides using those experiences, he bases his plots and characters on what he learned listening to student problems in the years he taught high school chemistry.

When he quit teaching Paul Zindel began to put all his observations and insights to work and started writing. The result has been a series of zany novels which are reaching an ever-growing audience of teenagers.

Zindel lives in Manhattan with his wife and two children. His latest book, THE UNDERTAKER'S GONE BANANAS, has just been published in hardcover by Harper & Row.

Meet Paul Zindel in all the books published by Bantam Books. Now available wherever paperbacks are sold.

MS READ-a-thon—
a simple way
to start youngsters reading.

Boys and girls between 6 and 14 can join the MS READ-a-thon and help find a cure for Multiple Sclerosis by reading books. And they get two rewards—the enjoyment of reading, and the great feeling that comes from helping others.

Parents and educators: For complete information call your local MS chapter, or call toll-free (800) 243-6000. Or mail the coupon below.

Kids can help, too!

Mail to:
National Multiple Sclerosis Society
205 East 42nd Street
New York, N.Y 10017

I would like more information about the MS READ-a-thon and how it can work in my area.

Name_____
            (please print)
Address_____
City_____State_____Zip_____
Organization_____
                              BA—10/77

TEENAGERS FACE LIFE AND LOVE

Choose books filled with fun and adventure, discovery and disenchantment, failure and conquest, triumph and tragedy, life and love.

☐	13359	**THE LATE GREAT ME** Sandra Scoppettone	$1.95
☐	13691	**HOME BEFORE DARK** Sue Ellen Bridgers	$1.75
☐	13671	**ALL TOGETHER NOW** Sue Ellen Bridgers	$1.95
☐	14836	**PARDON ME, YOU'RE STEPPING ON MY EYEBALL!** Paul Zindel	$2.25
☐	11091	**A HOUSE FOR JONNIE O.** Blossom Elfman	$1.95
☐	14306	**ONE FAT SUMMER** Robert Lipsyte	$1.95
☐	14690	**THE CONTENDER** Robert Lipsyte	$2.25
☐	13315	**CHLORIS AND THE WEIRDOS** Linn Platt	$1.95
☐	12577	**GENTLEHANDS** M. E. Kerr	$1.95
☐	12650	**QUEEN OF HEARTS** Bill & Vera Cleaver	$1.75
☐	12741	**MY DARLING, MY HAMBURGER** Paul Zindel	$1.95
☐	13555	**HEY DOLLFACE** Deborah Hautzig	$1.75
☐	13897	**WHERE THE RED FERN GROWS** Wilson Rawls	$2.25
☐	20170	**CONFESSIONS OF A TEENAGE BABOON** Paul Zindel	$2.25
☐	14730	**OUT OF LOVE** Hilma Wolitzer	$1.75
☐	14225	**SOMETHING FOR JOEY** Richard E. Peck	$2.25
☐	14687	**SUMMER OF MY GERMAN SOLDIER** Bette Greene	$2.25
☐	13693	**WINNING** Robin Brancato	$1.95

Buy them at your local bookstore or use this handy coupon for ordering

Bantam Books, Inc., Dept. EDN, 414 East Golf Road, Des Plaines, Ill. 60016

Please send me the books I have checked above. I am enclosing $_____ (please add $1.00 to cover postage and handling). Send check or money order —no cash or C.O.D.'s please.

Mr/Mrs/Miss _____

Address _____

City _____ State/Zip _____

EDN—7/81

Please allow four to six weeks for delivery. This offer expires 1/82.

DAHL, ZINDEL, BLUME AND BRANCATO

Select the best names, the best stories in the world of teenage and young readers books!

☐	20250	CHARLIE AND THE CHOCOLATE FACTORY Roald Dahl	$2.25
☐	20206	CHARLIE AND THE GREAT GLASS ELEVATOR Roald Dahl	$2.25
☐	12153	DANNY THE CHAMPION OF THE WORLD Roald Dahl	$1.95
☐	20172	THE UNDERTAKER'S GONE BANANAS Paul Zindel	$2.25
☐	12154	THE WONDERFUL STORY OF HENRY SUGAR AND SIX MORE Roald Dahl	$1.95
☐	14657	THE PIGMAN Paul Zindel	$2.25
☐	12774	I NEVER LOVED YOUR MIND Paul Zindel	$1.95
☐	14836	PARDON ME, YOU'RE STEPPING ON MY EYEBALL! Paul Zindel	$2.25
☐	12741	MY DARLING, MY HAMBURGER Paul Zindel	$1.95
☐	20170	CONFESSIONS OF A TEENAGE BABOON Paul Zindel	$2.25
☐	13628	IT'S NOT THE END OF THE WORLD Judy Blume	$1.95
☐	13693	WINNING Robin Brancato	$1.95
☐	12171	SOMETHING LEFT TO LOSE Robin Brancato	$1.75
☐	12953	BLINDED BY THE LIGHT Robin Brancato	$1.95

Buy them at your local bookstore or use this handy coupon for ordering:

Bantam Books, Inc., Dept. DA, 414 East Golf Road, Des Plaines, Ill. 60016

Please send me the books I have checked above. I am enclosing $_____ (please send $1.00 to cover postage and handling). Send check or money order —no cash or C.O.D.'s please.

Mr/Mrs/Miss_____

Address_____

City_____ State/Zip_____

DA—9/81

Please allow four to six weeks for delivery. This offer expires 11/81.

SAVE $2.00 ON YOUR NEXT BOOK ORDER!

BANTAM BOOKS

Shop-at-Home
Catalog

Now you can have a complete, up-to-date catalog of Bantam's inventory of over 1,600 titles—including hard-to-find books.

And, you can save $2.00 on your next order by taking advantage of the money-saving coupon you'll find in this illustrated catalog. Choose from fiction and non-fiction titles, including mysteries, historical novels, westerns, cookbooks, romances, biographies, family living, health, and more. You'll find a description of most titles. Arranged by categories, the catalog makes it easy to find your favorite books and authors and to discover new ones.

So don't delay—send for this shop-at-home catalog and save money on your next book order.

Just send us your name and address and 50¢ to defray postage and handling costs.

BANTAM BOOKS, INC.
Dept. FC, 414 East Golf Road, Des Plaines, Ill. 60016

Mr./Mrs./Miss_____
_____(please print)_____
Address_____

City_____State_____Zip_____

Do you know someone who enjoys books? Just give us their names and addresses and we'll send them a catalog too at no extra cost!

Mr./Mrs./Miss_____
Address_____

City_____State_____Zip_____

Mr./Mrs./Miss_____
Address_____

City_____State_____Zip_____

FC—8/81